ACADEMY OF THE FORSAKEN

CURSED STUDIES BOOK TWO

EVA CHASE

CHAPTER ONE

Trix

*H*ave you ever experienced déjà vu—the sense that you've lived through a specific moment before, even though you know it isn't possible?

I hadn't. But looking across the campus lawn toward Roseborne College as damp spring air laced with the scent of roses licked over my skin, I had a feeling like that ten times over.

I'd walked up the gravel path in front of me to that looming Victorian mansion more than once. I'd been here what felt like just a couple of weeks ago, full of the determination to get answers about my foster brother's disappearance. At the time, I'd thought I'd just arrived.

That had been a lie. Beneath my clearer memories of my last venture through Roseborne, fragments of other arrivals, other defiant marches up to the front of the school building, drifted through my mind. I couldn't tell how many different versions of these first minutes on campus I'd been through. All I knew for sure was that it wasn't déjà vu, some inexplicable but unreliable sensation. I really *had* lived through this exact moment several if not dozens of times before.

This time, this once, I remembered.

I dragged in a breath to steady myself. My lungs flooded with the floral odor that wafted off the rosebush that clung to the entire stone wall surrounding the campus, even though the actual blooms were sparse. After everything I'd been through here, it wasn't exactly a comforting smell, but it reminded me of how much was at stake here—not just for me but every student in the place. How careful would I have to be if I wanted to save any of us from the staff and their unnerving powers?

Forcing my hands to relax at my sides, I strode up the gravel path to the imposing building. I half expected Jenson to come sauntering out with more of the caustic remarks he'd thrown my way on my last arrival, but no one emerged from the school at all. The front steps creaked under my combat boots, and the door squeaked open at my tug.

A few students ambled through the foyer as I came in, the planes of their faces turned harsh by the light of the chandelier overhead. One of the girls glanced my way and let out an audible sigh. The guy beside her rolled his eyes without even fully looking at me.

They obviously knew I'd failed yet another attempt at unraveling the college's mysteries, at least as far as the staff were concerned. They assumed I was going to go through the same motions of searching for my foster brother and being baffled by the school's practices as I always had before when I hadn't remembered.

But I knew where Cade was now. I knew about the emotional and physical torment the professors dealt out on a whim. I knew their powers were somehow tied to a twisted, blossom-less rosebush that was reverberating with unsettling energy in the secret basement beneath our feet.

If I showed that I knew any of that, the staff would realize their most recent attempt to wipe my memories and reset my progress here hadn't stuck. Lord only knew what shit they'd put me through then. No, I'd much rather leave them in ignorance while I figured out how to best screw them over.

I could already see one change had been made in light of my most recent attempt at unraveling the school's secrets. The matching suits of armor still stood, gleaming, at either side of the grand staircase that led to the second floor, but their metal chests were bare. Someone had removed the massive shields they'd held the last—and presumably every other—time I'd been here. I guessed I wouldn't be using that trick to bash through the padlocked basement door again.

I let my gaze skim over them and settle on the door to the dean's office at my left. That was where I'd started my search before. If I hadn't known that Dean Wainhouse was a malicious, not-quite-human prick, it was where I'd have turned again. Since I was pretending I didn't know that, what else was there to do? I stepped up to the door and knocked.

The dean answered a few moments later and peered down at me over his hooked nose in an uncomfortably familiar pose. His pale skin held a silvery tint that matched the hair slicked back from his forehead. That tint had shone starker on both him and the professors when they'd surrounded me in the foyer last night.

My pulse stuttered as that image flashed through my mind, but I forced my mouth into a hopeful smile. "Hi! I'm Beatrix Corbyn. I'm looking for my brother."

"Your brother?" Dean Wainhouse repeated, his brow furrowing. Apparently he was content to go through the motions of pretending *he* didn't know my story already. Didn't he get as bored with this charade as the students did?

I'd just have to keep playing along. "Cade Harrison," I said. "He got a spot here on scholarship, came at the beginning of the school year."

There was that slight hint of a grimace, there and gone so quickly I almost missed it. The dean pushed the door farther. "Come in, and I'll see what I can tell you. I'm Dean Wainhouse, and I handle student affairs here at Roseborne College."

I already knew how this would go too. He'd make a show of asking a few more questions, tell me he had no idea who the hell Cade was, and send me on my way. I'd just have to see if I could get anything more out of this interaction without him noticing how purposeful I was being.

Stepping into the large room with its sitting area and broad oak desk, I glanced around as if taking in the space for the first time. Actually, I was checking for any details I might have missed the few times I remembered getting a look at the space before. Were there any secrets tucked away in here that I hadn't uncovered?

The puzzle box on the desk caught my eye like it had once before. Hmm. Today, my very "first" day here, I could get away with more in feigned innocence than I'd be able to later.

As the dean tossed off a few remarks and questions about Cade's supposed enrollment, I gave my answers by rote and eased closer to the desk. In a casual gesture, I picked up the puzzle box and turned it over, my fingers tracing the lines in the varnished wood, feeling for pressure points.

"Pretty cool," I said, as if I was looking at it out of idle curiosity and nothing more. Through my lowered eyelashes, I checked the dean's expression.

Nothing in his face suggested he was concerned about what I might find there, and I didn't hear anything shift inside the box. Maybe it was empty, a diversion and nothing more.

"Yes," he said. "I inherited it from the dean before me. I'm afraid I can't tell you more than I already have about your brother. If he attended classes here, I'm sure I'd know."

Same old story, same old lies. I set the puzzle box down, resisting the urge to chuck it at his falsely apologetic smile. "Can I check around a little, talk with some of the students and see if any of them saw him come by?" I asked. I needed to set up the groundwork for why I was sticking around.

The dean lowered his head in a stiff bob. "That's acceptable, as long as you don't interrupt anyone's work."

"Thank you."

One hurdle crossed. I emerged into the foyer with a creeping sensation spreading over my skin as I held back all the comments I'd have liked to hurl at the guy. *I know what a sick asshole you are. You're not fooling me anymore.*

Maybe I should be grateful for the years upon years with asshole foster parents who'd quickly taught me that it was better to keep your mouth shut about your complaints unless you were in a position to actually hit back. I managed to hold my tongue.

Soon. Roseborne's staff wouldn't get away with the horrors they orchestrated here forever.

My feet carried me a little farther down the hall to the row of portraits that hung there. The one with Cade's subtle signature, the sketchy starburst that matched the birthmark on his arm and the scar I'd cut into my own arm years ago to match, remained untouched. I studied the figures in the paintings—different types of paint, different styles, but with each of the four young men and three young women depicted wearing the same burgundy jackets over white dress shirts.

I'd seen them before in another way, hadn't I? Down in the hidden basement in the room that held the warped rosebush, there'd been photographs fixed to the wall. I hadn't gotten a close look at them in the wavering light, but they'd been wearing the same uniform. The only difference was there'd been eight down there and only seven portraits stood before me up here, although the faint discoloration on the wood paneling at the end suggested there might have been another hung there before.

Who *were* those people? Past students from a time when the college had insisted on uniforms? What did they have to do with the weird powers that infected the campus?

Before I could think very much about that, sneakered feet murmured across the floor. "New here?" the boy who'd joined me said in a mellow voice with a slightly hoarse undertone, familiar and much more welcome than anything else I'd recognized yet. "You look a little lost."

I had to restrain the grin that wanted to leap to my lips as I turned to face him. The sight of Ryo Shibata's boyishly soft features, made edgier by the silver eyebrow ring and the bright green streaks that shot through his smooth black hair, sent a flutter through my chest. The flutter set off a nervous jolt in turn.

Ryo had been the only student here who'd been friendly from the start of my last few weeks navigating this place—friendly and sweet, and passionate when he decided to be with an intensity that gleamed in those golden eyes. From the wisps of memories that had reached me from further back, he'd stood by me and tried to make the horrors of the college easier to cope with a whole lot more times than that.

From what I'd gathered, Roseborne collected students with some sort of destructive past. I didn't know what crime had brought Ryo here or what his punishment for that crime was, but he cared about me… and I'd started to care about him. More than I should? How much could I truly count on him when he didn't really know *me*?

I shoved those questions aside and smiled back at him with a restrained warmth that I hoped would look normal to anyone watching. Everyone around us would assume that as far as I could remember, he was a stranger. *He* wouldn't expect me to remember him either.

"I am new, actually," I said. "Maybe you could give me a hand?"

Ryo's eyebrows twitched slightly upward. Maybe he'd caught something in my expression that suggested I was more aware than I was letting on. I needed to talk to him —to the few people here who'd proven they were willing to help me—if I was going to have a real chance of overcoming the beings that ruled this school. I could handle a hell of a lot, but I wasn't naïve enough to think I could overthrow a bunch of supernatural dictators all on my own.

"Sure," Ryo said easily. "What did you need a hand with? I could show you around the school if you'd like."

Yes. We needed a place to talk where the staff weren't likely to overhear. This building wasn't really secure. The possibilities flitted through my mind.

The carriage house. Pretty much no one ever used that, from what I'd seen.

I kept my tone innocent. "You know, I was curious about that building off to the right of the school—the one that looks like some kind of old-fashioned garage? Could you show me how to get in there?"

"Not a problem." He motioned for me to follow him, studying me with even more curiosity than before. If he did suspect that something was up, he knew better than to press the subject here.

He led me out of the mansion and across the lawn to the long building with its three wide doors that would have admitted carriages a long time ago. I didn't really need Ryo to escort me—the entrance wasn't locked and opened easily at his nudge—but it bought us the privacy I wanted.

Ryo turned to consider me as the door clicked shut behind us. In the dim space with the aroma of old wood and leather rising around us to cut through the ever-present roses, I couldn't stop my mind from slipping back to more intimate moments we'd shared here. Just last night, we'd fucked on one of those padded benches. From the glimpses I'd gotten into previous journeys through this place, that hadn't been the first time, even though I'd thought it was at the time. It'd been good. It'd been exactly what I'd needed.

Without letting myself second-guess the impulse, I stepped forward, set my hand against his cheek, and kissed him.

CHAPTER TWO

Trix

Ryo's breath stuttered in surprise against my mouth, and then he was kissing me back hard, his fingers tangling in my hair as if he thought that would help him hold me here. A sharper heat sparked low in my belly, but now wasn't the time to get overly distracted. After a moment, I forced myself to pull back.

His eyes gleamed even brighter than before as he stared at me. "Trix?" he said, both hopeful and hesitant to give more voice to that hope.

"I didn't win the day, but I beat them a little this time," I said. "There's a lot I need to tell you. But not just you. Can you find some excuse to get Jenson and Elias out here?"

Ryo beamed at me, so brilliantly another of those flutters passed through my chest. "I'm sure I can figure something out." He paused, as if he couldn't quite tear his gaze away from me. "It's good—so good—to have you really here."

My voice came out quiet. "For me too."

He hurried out, and I wandered farther into the carriage house. The main hall down the middle of the building held a few of those leather-padded benches, but I felt too restless to sit down. Eagerness and uncertainty clashed inside me at the thought of seeing the other two guys who'd helped me in their own ways. Who'd offered me a sort of devotion that was only just starting to make sense.

The three of them returned together, but Jenson took the lead. He strode into the carriage house in mid-sentence: "—understand why I might not totally trust your judgment?"

His coolly confident voice trailed off when he caught sight of me. He came to a halt, his bright blue eyes fixed on my face, his tall, slim form held with his typical nonchalance. The artful scruffiness of his cinnamon-brown hair and the slight crook to his nose gave him a roguish air that he wore well.

"I'm back," I said, the corners of my lips quirking upward as I waited for his full reaction. "With a lot more of my mind than they think they left me with."

My recent associations with Jenson Wynter could best be described as "chaotic." The last time I'd made my arrival at Roseborne, from the moment I'd approached the school, he'd begun a campaign to try to harass me into leaving. But here and there a playfulness had started to come out between the barbed jabs, and eventually he'd been able to make it clear that he'd been an asshole in an attempt to protect me from the torture the college subjected its students to.

The bits I remembered from times before only reinforced that revelation—while leaving me with more questions this didn't feel like the right time to ask.

Jenson blinked at me, and then a smirk stretched across his face that was nothing less than triumphant. "Holy fuck," he said. "Look at you. Wait until those pricks find out they messed with the wrong girl."

The third guy in our strange sort-of coalition had come up beside Jenson. With his buff, broad-shouldered frame wrapped in one of his usual suits, Elias DeLeon gave the impression of someone to be reckoned with before he so much as opened his mouth. His expression stayed stern as he took in my exchange with Jenson, his dark brown eyes alert with thought.

"They don't know," he suggested as soon as Jenson had spoken. "The staff. That's why we're meeting out here— you're hoping they won't find out."

He'd mentioned to me, last time and in snippets from times before, that he'd been something of a business prodigy—and a cutthroat one—in his life before the college. The strategic precision that success must have entailed came across in how easily he'd pieced together the current situation.

I nodded, relieved that I didn't need to explain that one point. I wasn't entirely sure where I stood with the guy who was both a student here and acting math teacher. He'd gone out of his way to avoid me for most of the last two weeks... but he'd ended up doing more to help me unravel the mysteries around the school than anyone else had managed, while also admitting some sort of attraction to me. An attraction I had the sense we'd acted on at least once in earlier run-throughs of my time at Roseborne.

"From what they said, I got farther than I ever have before," I said. "And this is the first time I've been able to hold onto any memories of being here—at least, I think it is. How... how many times has it been?"

Ryo offered me a pained smile. "This would be number eight, if I've counted right. And until now, you've never shown you had any idea you'd been through this before."

Elias inclined his head in agreement.

That wasn't as bad as I'd been afraid of, really. Still a hell of a lot more missing time than I'd have wanted to face, but I'd been prepared to hear I'd been fumbling through this cycle unknowingly for years. Seven previous cycles was more like a few months, assuming the previous ones had gone on for about as long as the most recent ordeal.

"How much exactly do you remember?" Jenson asked. He'd propped himself against the wooden wall in a stance that should have looked laidback, but the tension in his shoulders indicated he was far from at ease. Because he didn't like to think of how much of his crappy behavior I might remember?

"The last time is totally clear in my head," I said. "The same way I remember things from before I came here. The rest—it's more like fragments and impressions. I don't know what happened when or how they all connect." I glanced around at the three of them. "I guess you guys can help me figure that out if anything comes to mind that seems important."

"Of course," Ryo said. "Anything you need."

Elias was still studying me with his penetrating gaze. "What happened last night? I know you were planning on trying something against the staff... Whenever they send you back to the start of this whole process, there's a sort of wave of energy that rushes through the school. I didn't notice that it felt any different from before."

Ah. That explained why everyone expected me to start out the day acting clueless again. My hand rose instinctively to the starburst scar on my arm, tracing the thin lines as if they could defend me from the awful scene I'd stumbled into just hours ago.

"There's a door at the end of the hall with the staff's rooms," I said. "It's labeled *Bushfell*. I don't know if you've noticed it?"

"I figured that was a professor who just wasn't around anymore," Ryo said. "There are a couple of names that don't fit anyone I've met at the school."

I shook my head. "It leads down to a second, larger basement area. I managed to break in, and I found what I have to think is the source of the staff's power here. There was a huge room with a rosebush growing out of the floor, but all twisted up with no flowers and thorns way longer and sharper than any regular plant... And it had what looked like mementos from students who've died caught all over it. I saw a lock of Delta's hair."

One of my roommates had passed away yesterday evening, wasted and weak as if the school had drained all the life from her. We hadn't exactly been friends, but she'd offered me a little advice. The memory of her gaunt, vacant face made my stomach clench up.

Ryo shuddered, and Jenson grimaced. "How the hell does a rosebush grow in a basement without any sunlight?"

Elias shot the other guy an irritated look. "That would obviously be the main sign that it's something supernatural."

"Not just that," I said. "This eerie energy came off it, all through the room. I could just tell there was power in it. There were also— Eight student photos were attached to the wall. I think they might be the same ones the portraits in the hall by the dean's office are based on. Do any of you know who those people are or what that's all about—or why there are only seven of them now?"

"It's an assignment given out in art class every now and then," Elias said. "The professor shows everyone photo references to work from. He's never explained why…"

"After a while here, you learn you're better off not asking too many questions," Ryo said, making a face. "They hardly ever answer anyway."

"Maybe those pictures or the people in them have something to do with the staff's power too." The images from that underground room swam up through my mind. "There were stains on the floor that looked like blood. Maybe the staff used those students in some kind of sacrifice to set everything in motion, who knows how long ago? The paintings might help keep their powers going."

"Do you really think breaking their hold could be as simple as destroying the portraits?" Jenson asked with obvious skepticism.

"No." My sense of the twisted rosebush's energy echoed through me. "Doing that might help, but I can't see it being enough to stop them on its own."

Ryo reached out to squeeze my hand. "You must have done something that got in the way of their power, or you wouldn't have held on to any of this."

"I—" *That* memory temporarily closed my throat. The anguish I'd felt over my brother's fate and my part in it, the stabbing sensation of the thorns slicing into my flesh. "The professors and the dean had all come after me. They told me about the cycles and started to send me back. The only thing I could think of to do was—I said the school should take me in Cade's place and threw myself at the bush on the thorns. I just hoped it would throw *something* off in the whole system they have going here."

I resisted the urge to hug myself as a tremor ran down my back. I'd been ready to die if it meant making up for what I'd done—what none of the guys around me had any idea I was capable of. They thought I was so much better than them…

All of them looked stricken by the lengths I'd gone to. Elias recovered first with a thoughtful frown. "Something about that act must have interfered with their powers, or we wouldn't be having this conversation."

"They've never been able to totally control Trix," Ryo

said, and met my eyes. "You said everyone who knew your brother forgot he'd ever existed—that you figure the same thing happened to the people who'd have known all of us, which is why no one wonders why we're stuck at the college or comes looking for us. But *you* remembered Cade. They weren't able to wipe him from your mind."

That was true, but— "I have no idea why."

"Don't you think that's why they haven't kicked her out?" Jenson said abruptly. "Why else would they let her stay at Roseborne when she's peeling away their secrets?"

Ryo nodded slowly. "They know that if they tried to send her away, she'd still remember Cade and this place. She might make even more trouble for them from outside. They were going to let her leave this time, though."

Thinking of the dean's proposal, I swallowed thickly. "I only agreed because they managed to convince me that I *couldn't* help anyone here, not even Cade. I started to think I was only making things worse. If I'd left with that mindset, maybe their magic would have worked on me."

"But you didn't give up," Elias said. "There will be answers—we just have to find them. That's why you called us all here, isn't it? So we can come up with a plan going forward?"

A large part of me had just wanted to see them, to show them I'd made some kind of difference and to confirm for myself that I had allies here. But having three more sets of eyes and ears on my side would be awfully useful.

"I'd like to get back into that basement and take a more careful look around if I can," I said. "That would be easier if we can get our hands on a key for it. And I want to find out more about the students from the portraits and how they fit into the whole situation. Other than that, anything we can observe about how the staff function—weaknesses they might have, or things they need before they can work certain powers—could help too. I know that's all pretty vague…"

"It's a starting point," Ryo said, running his thumb over the back of my hand in an affectionate caress. "We'll see where it gets us."

His touch stirred up a totally different set of memories: our hasty hook-up last night, the kiss I'd shared with Jenson and the hug I'd given Elias, the snippets of more distant pasts that showed a more intimate connection with all three of them. They'd all been invested in me more than I'd understood when I'd "arrived" here last time. That thought was both thrilling and unnerving.

I wet my lips. "Maybe there's something else we should talk about before we go all Nancy Drew and the Hardy Boys on this place. I—I don't remember exactly how it all happened the times before, but I know I ended up getting involved with each of you at least once. I had no idea at the time—I wasn't trying to jerk anyone around—"

Ryo's fingers tightened where they were twined with mine. "Of course you weren't. None of us thought that."

For a moment, Jenson looked twice as tense as before, his mouth twisting, but then he shrugged and managed to pull off a slanted smile and a blasé tone. "Who says you owe anyone anything? It's no big deal."

He caught himself with a tightening of his jaw as he must have realized his mistake. Yesterday, he'd conveyed to me the only way he could what curse Roseborne had laid on him—he couldn't say anything true. Most of the time he resorted to questions and commands when he needed to get a point across, but any direct statement he gave was a lie.

The fact that *we'd* hooked up some time in the past mattered a lot more than he'd wanted to say.

"We can all be adults about it," Elias said firmly. "If there's a way to get everyone free from this place, that matters a hell of a lot more than any romantic entanglement. It's not as if any of us are in a position to make some kind of commitment."

"Exactly," Ryo said. "We can just see where that goes too, as it comes up." He held my gaze. "I think you're wonderful, Trix, but mostly I want to see you happy. As far as I'm concerned, if that means turning to all three of us for whatever you want in that moment, there's no reason you should hold yourself back. Might as well make the most of what we do have here." He waggled his eyebrows and then shot a look at the other two as if daring them to argue.

His words sent a tingle through me that I liked more than I was totally at ease with. Jenson pushed himself off the wall. "Sure," he said, and caught my eyes. "Do what you want. Now why don't we get on with the important stuff?"

CHAPTER THREE

Jenson

I might have regretted some of the things I'd done in the past serving the principles I'd grown up with, but I still believed in a few of the lessons I'd gotten from my parents. For starters, if you found yourself more off-balance than you could adjust for in the moment, you were much better off making a quick excuse to get out and regroup than barreling ahead on shaky ground.

I meant to take that advice to heart with the wrap-up of our little meeting with Trix. But before I could take my leave with Elias and Ryo, Trix caught my arm. The warmth of her hand bled straight through the thin fabric of my button-up shirt and sent a deeper heat rippling through me that only stirred up the emotions I'd been trying to settle down.

"Hey," she said, fixing me with those light green eyes

that had always been more perceptive than I'd liked. "Can we talk for a minute, just you and me?"

No. Bad idea. I didn't think I could trust what might come out of my mouth or show on my face. I'd already put my foot in it once, however much she'd realized that, and I'd been more abrasive in general than I'd have preferred to be. Bold but smooth was the proper approach when you wanted things to go your way. But these days being around the other two guys sharpened my temper, and being around Trix opened up raw spots better left undisturbed. Both factors in combination was a disastrous recipe for my self-control.

I couldn't give her *that* excuse, though, and what other good one did I have? She'd know anything I could say was bullshit. Why oh why had I thought it was a good idea to demonstrate my curse to her?

"Why not?" I said with a casual shrug. Ryo shot me a smile that looked slightly amused as he brushed past us. I held myself back from glowering at him.

It'd been easy for *him* to talk about "making the most of what we had" when it came to our shared interest in Trix. He was the one she'd turned to almost every time; he had the confidence of that history. He probably figured no matter what had happened or happened again with Elias and me, he could count on her turning to him when it really mattered. And given that he barely seemed to give a shit about anything or anyone in general, why should he care what she got up to with anyone else in the meantime as long as he got what he wanted in the end?

Not that I was planning on getting up to anything

along those lines with Trix ever again. Even if the brush of her lips against mine last night was burned into my memory alongside the more distant moments we'd shared before. I'd learned that lesson too.

As the door swung shut behind the other guys, Trix stepped back to the other side of the hall to give me space. Or to give herself space? I couldn't tell. She swiped her fingers through her artificially bright orange hair to sweep it behind her ear and sucked her lower lip under her teeth, just for an instant, before she met my eyes again. A brief hint of vulnerability from this girl who rarely let anyone get to her.

Was she nervous about what I'd say now that it was just the two of us in the vacant building? Only thin light streamed through the narrow windows at either end of the hall, and the tang of the aging leather tack hanging on the walls made my nose itch. The momentary silence crept over my skin. Why *wouldn't* she be nervous, when the clearest memories she'd have of me would mostly be of me trying to shame her into leaving Roseborne?

Only with her, impatience got the better of me. "What is it, Trix?" I asked, folding my arms over my chest. At least I managed to keep my tone mild rather than accusing.

"I just—we haven't really had a chance to talk—" She cut herself off with a sound of frustration as if she were struggling as much to get the right words out as I often had to around my curse. Her shoulders squared. "Ryo's always been pretty clear about where I stand with him, and Elias has told me enough that I think I understand where he was coming from. But you... You came at me right from the start last time, with all the taunts and insults."

"Didn't I make it clear enough that I just wanted you to get out of here while you could, before the assholes who run this place could screw you over like they do us?"

Her eyes narrowed at my deflection. "*You* didn't have to be a total asshole about it. Maybe I can't remember the times I've gone through this cycle before that very clearly, but the bits I do remember—I don't think you ever went after me like that before. I get the impression we enjoyed each other's company pretty well."

Enjoyed each other's company. That was one way of putting it. How much could she tell from the bits of memories she had? The bantering conversations where she somehow ended up drawing more truth out of me than I'd known I was capable of expressing? The two heart-wrenchingly short encounters when we'd outright collided in a blaze of heat that felt almost desperate?

One time, her path here at Roseborne had crossed with mine in just the right way, and I'd been hooked. Just one time. I convinced myself at the time it was all in good fun, making the most of this godawful situation while we could, like Ryo had said. And then seeing her gaze pass over me with no recognition just a couple of days later, watching her fall back into old habits with Ryo and then, of all the pricks in this place, the stuffed shirt that was Elias...

I looked at her, imagining the words that would answer the question she hadn't quite asked. *I never let myself care about anyone I got close to before. I never let myself do anything more than pretend to get close in the first place. And that was fucking smart, because caring and then losing is like having your guts cut out with a rusty knife.*

Why would I want to go through that again? Even if she wouldn't forget next time, which we couldn't really assume, it wasn't as if I deserved *her* caring in the first place.

The best place for her was still on the other side of the campus walls, as far as she could get from all us sorry souls incarcerated in here. And if waving goodbye to her meant shielding myself from an agony the staff had nothing on, who could blame me for being on board with that side effect?

I grappled with the words to get across as much of that as I was willing to admit to. "How selfish would I be if I gave you reasons to stick around this hellhole instead of reasons to take off?" I said. "What am I supposed to do other than make use of the resources I have?"

"Resources like the ability to make someone feel like crap for trying to do the right thing?" She studied me, her eyes turning more alert by the second. "You knew exactly what jabs to throw at me for maximum impact, didn't you? I thought you were making good guesses from a few observations, but you had the benefit of who knows how much history to mine for material."

When she put it that way, yes, I sounded like the biggest prick that ever walked the earth. I shifted my weight, shaping my next comments with just as much care. My curse would let me get away with orders as well as questions as long as I didn't push them so far they turned back into outright statements of fact. "Don't look at it that way. Look at it as me giving my attempt to save you all the effort I could."

"It wouldn't really have saved me, though. If I'd gone through with leaving and let myself give up—" She stopped and shook her head. "If you're so sure it was the right approach, why did you change your tune in the end?"

Because it hadn't been working. Because I'd realized that being a jerk was more about protecting myself than her.

And maybe because I'd wanted her to look at me one more time like she had in the infirmary right before she'd kissed me. I couldn't say I'd really stopped being selfish even in the end.

"And how much did *that* approach help anything either?" I said rather than answering as I shoved down the prickling uneasiness. "Aren't you still here? Do you have any idea what they're going to do to you if they find out you gave them the slip?"

"Do you really wish I was gone and you all were stuck with the same horrible situation?"

Yes, I wanted to say. *I wish I never saw your lovely face again except in my imagination, picturing you having a real life out there.* But the fact that I could say that would only betray that it was a lie. I did wish that... while also wishing I never had to give her up at all.

"Wouldn't I be an even worse asshole if I wanted you stuck here with us?" I asked instead.

"No," she said quietly. "I think that would just make you human."

Something inside me clenched up at the sympathy in her words. She was trying to understand me, trying to know me in ways that wouldn't benefit either of us—but she wanted to anyway.

Maybe I'd perpetuated a greater con here than I'd let myself suspect.

"Keep in mind that you don't really know that much about me," I said. "Save that concern for yourself."

A rough laugh spilled out of her. "And how much do you know about me?"

Enough. More than enough to be sure she didn't belong here. "Trix," I said, not sure where to go from there. The strands of the conversation seemed to have twisted around on themselves into an even bigger mess than when we'd started.

"Are you even going to help with all the stuff we talked about?" she asked with a jerky motion toward the space where we'd all stood talking ten minutes ago. "Or would that be too helpful for you to stomach? Should I expect that in another day or two you might change your mind again and go back to hassling me at every opportunity?"

"What would be the point in that when you'd see right through it?"

"So you would have started up again if I'd forgotten everything like you expected?"

A thread I hadn't even realized was fraying inside me snapped. "Yes. Of course! I'd have laid into you like there was no tomorrow because it's so much fun trying to tear you down, and I definitely enjoyed every second of it the last time around, and I don't give a shit what happens to you as long as I get my kicks in. That's why I'm here right now, because I've got no interest at all in doing anything to support you."

I regretted the words the second they'd tumbled out. Trix was already wincing, but not for the reason she would have been if she hadn't known enough about me to read between the lines. To know the fact that I'd said all that meant the opposite was true.

"I'm sorry," she said, her voice tight. "I shouldn't be making accusations or asking for more when you've already— I know you've been trying. It's just been hard to wrap my head around all of this. I'm not good at believing people even when they *can* give me straight answers. You shouldn't feel badgered into taking more risks for me out of guilt or whatever."

She turned with a whirl of that bright hair, and my heart lurched. Without thinking, I sprang forward and caught her wrist. "Trix," I said as she turned back toward me. I stepped closer. "Don't. Don't."

What was I telling her not to do? I wasn't even sure. Nothing I could say felt adequate. That was the only excuse I could give for why I found myself slipping my fingers along her jaw and bowing my head to capture her mouth.

How could kissing her feel so much better than any other girl I'd ever been with, and yet so terrifying at the same time? The heat of her mouth sent an electric shock through me. My heart hammered at my ribs.

I was going to lose her. I was going to lose her all over again. Every nerve in my body clanged with that warning, but for that moment, I couldn't bring myself to listen. The heady rush of it was too wonderful to give up.

When I eased back an inch, she was gripping my shirt. She gazed up at me with both a question and a hunger I had to draw on every ounce of discipline not to answer.

"Did that feel like guilt to you?" I asked in a low voice.

"No," she said with a soft quirk of her lips. "Point taken."

At least she sounded convinced. I still couldn't tell whether it'd been the best move I'd ever made—or the worst.

CHAPTER FOUR

Trix

Roseborne's art classes were taught by Professor Filch, a grayed, hulking man whose body appeared to be constructed entirely out of rectangles. His head might as well have been a cinderblock for all the expression he offered with it. His pale eyes somehow managed to look both watery and emotionless.

After he answered my knock on the art room door, he considered me with those eyes for a long moment. I'd made my usual deal with the staff where they let me stick around and keep up my search for information about Cade as long as I acted as a full student, pretending I thought it was the first time I'd ever asked. I'd even picked an unused bed in a different bedroom from last time, partly to play into the ruse that I didn't know there'd been a last time and partly because the thought of returning to the room where I'd watched Delta waste away made me queasy. But art wasn't on my current class schedule until next week, so I was dropping in on Filch uninvited.

"Yes, Miss…?" he said in a hollow voice that only emphasized the cinderblock impression. The earthy scent of clay drifted past him from the room beyond.

I smiled at him with a concentrated effort not to grit my teeth. He knew exactly what my name was, but I wasn't supposed to know *that*.

"Corbyn," I said as politely as I could manage. "This is the art room, right? I had a question about, well, art."

The man's eyebrows managed to stay straight across even as he lifted them. "I suppose you've come to the right place, then." He didn't move to let me into the room.

I gestured vaguely toward the stairs to the first floor. "Those painted portraits that are hanging in the hall downstairs—someone told me they were done by students here. I was just wondering who the people in them are. No one around here seems to wear uniforms like that."

Professor Filch smiled thinly. "They're students from decades past who contributed a great deal to making this college what it is today. We honor them with an art contest every year in which the best renditions are hung as you've seen them."

"Contributed" to making the college, huh? *That* didn't sound ominous at all. I willed my face to look awed rather than unsettled. "That's pretty cool. When's the contest going to happen again?" If Cade had been himself enough to participate, it couldn't have been very long into his stay here. After seven past cycles of arriving and searching for him, it had to be coming up on a year since he'd started here.

"Oh, not for a few months yet," Filch said without any hint of concern. "If you're still with us then, I suppose you'll get to try your hand at it as well."

"No chance of getting some early practice in?" I kept my tone light as if it were a joke, but Elias had said the professor gave photo references for the portraits. I'd like to get my hands on those photographs.

Filch chuckled, an equally hollow sound. "I'm afraid you'll have to be patient like the others."

Well, that hadn't gotten me very far. I meandered a little down the hall as he shut the door, and turned to eye it. I should be able to get in there the same way I'd made my way through other doors with regular locks around this place. A card placed at the right angle could pop the old-fashioned latch no problem. But the staff always seemed to sense whenever anyone was poking very far into places they weren't meant to be. The dean had caught me within a matter of minutes the one time I'd broken into his office. It'd be risky showing I was willing to go that far this soon.

Violet, one of my former roommates, walked past without a glance my way, her cloud of curls billowing around her face. I balked against the impulse to call after her. She hadn't exactly chummed up to me during my last time, but she had offered a couple of tips that had pointed me in the right direction... and confessed the horrible incident that had brought her here and left her with vicious burn scars down one side of her body from forehead to calf.

Did I really want to make friends with a girl who'd been willing to set off a bomb in her high school cafeteria over some of her classmates making fun of her clothes and hair?

Was I any better than her when I'd destroyed someone who'd never purposefully hurt me even on that small scale?

It didn't matter anyway. Now that we weren't sharing a bedroom in the dorms, she appeared to have decided there was no point in re-establishing whatever small connection we'd formed. I didn't think, from the impressions I had of my times here, that we'd really talked in the more distant past either.

A few other girls wandered by with muttered remarks when they noticed me. Other than my three guys, none of the students had bothered to talk to me since I'd shown up, but that much was business as usual. Why care about the perpetually new girl and her annoying questions? I was only trying to save all of them from years of torment.

I swallowed that annoyance and headed down for my shift on laundry duty. At least I wouldn't have Jenson heckling me through my work this time.

The staff kept a close watch over the school building, but they hadn't shown signs of being as sensitive to what went on beyond its walls. That was why I'd called the guys over to the carriage house to speak, and why I let out my breath in relief the second I slipped out the front door at midnight to make my way into the woods that sprawled across the south end of campus.

As I hurried across the lawn under the hazy light of the moon, half covered by the clouds that never totally left the sky over the college, a knot of tension returned to my stomach. I might have escaped notice by the staff, but I had a different sort of reckoning ahead of me.

It'd taken nearly two weeks of my last cycle at Roseborne, but Ryo and Elias had finally told me enough that I'd discovered my foster brother's fate. Cade was still on campus, but not really at the *school*. For months, he'd been living in these woods, trapped in the shape of a horrifying monster nearly all of the time.

Ryo had said that at first he'd only transformed for short periods, and he'd been able to attend classes then. These days... Elias had indicated that I'd be able to find Cade in human form at half-past midnight. It couldn't have been much later than that when I'd managed to meet him after I'd gone searching for him, and I didn't think we'd been together more than fifteen minutes before the change had come over him again.

In those fifteen minutes, I'd admitted to him that it'd been my careless plan to scare his girlfriend that had gotten her killed. A crime only compounded by the fact that I'd let my own fears keep me silent while he'd blamed a guy who'd hassled her before and beat him into a coma in retaliation. That show of rage had to be why the beings that ran Roseborne had decided he deserved to be here—

and it never would have happened if I hadn't lost my mind to petty jealousy.

I hadn't gotten a chance to see how Cade would respond to that revelation. He'd started to shift into his monstrous form somewhere in the middle of my confession. Tonight, I'd have to face the music.

Ever since I'd come to stay with my second foster family when I was seven and Cade eight, he'd stood up for me, comforted me, been there for me in every possible way. He'd managed to keep us together across two more transfers to new families, and we'd planned to get an apartment together once we'd saved up enough to leave the last of those. I'd never been able to count on anyone in my life other than him. And now he might want me *out* of his life forever.

More knots twisted my gut as I picked my way between the trees, switching on the light of my phone to make it easier to see. He'd have a right to cut me out, I reminded myself. How could he count on *me* after what I'd done? How could he still care about me?

It didn't matter. I owed it to him to save him from this place. Even if *I* never left here, even if I ended up wasting away like the others, I had to get him out.

The forest grew denser around me. My heart thumped faster as I reached the area where I'd encountered Cade before—first as a hulking, coarse-furred beast with a row of fangs that jutted around his wolfish jaw, then as his real self. My phone's clock said it was exactly twelve-thirty. I stopped beneath the rustling leaves and sucked in a lungful of the cool night air.

"Cade?" I called into the stillness of the forest. My pulse counted out several seconds, and then footsteps crackled through the brush toward me.

My worries couldn't dampen the joy that rushed through me at the sight of the well-built figure with his mussed blond hair that emerged into the light. A few twigs and bits of leaf clung to Cade's thin sweater; a smudge of dirt marked his cheek. Here was an older version of the boy who'd liked to play rough and tumble in the ravine a couple of blocks from our first home together. Absolutely, completely himself—down to the crooked grin he gave me.

"You came back," he said. "I wasn't totally sure, after seeing what they've done to me…"

He hadn't been sure that *I'd* want to be around *him*? I'd already seen him transformed when Ryo had first brought me out here to show me my brother's fate. Cade didn't seem surprised that I'd known to come out here again at all, but Elias had said that the power the staff used to send me back to my arrival echoed through the school building. The impact might not carry all the way out into the woods.

"Of course I came," I said. "None of this is your fault."

He shrugged. "They seem to think it's suitable payback."

"But they don't know—they have it all wrong—" The words caught in the back of my mouth. Neither the words he'd said nor the way he was looking at me offered any indication that he remembered what I'd told him. I peered into his light gray eyes. "I tried to explain everything last time we talked."

Cade cocked his head. "What's there to explain, Baby Bea? I let my temper get the better of me, and the psychos who run this place decided to lay down their crazy judgment. You couldn't have stopped them."

I could have stopped it from happening in the first place by not setting the whole chain of events in motion. Sure, Cade's temper had always been unpredictable. How many jobs had he lost in the years before he'd come here because he'd blown up at some customer or coworker or even his boss? But that was just because he felt things so deeply. He'd never hurt anyone like he had Richie before.

Could he really have missed my whole confession, or was his refusal to acknowledge it his way of telling me it didn't matter to him? I couldn't tell. But my throat constricted against the thought of spilling my guts all over again. If he *did* remember, he obviously wanted to brush it aside. And if he didn't…

I'd tell him again. I'd make sure he understood exactly how horribly I'd fucked up. Just not right now. I'd have a better chance of getting him out if we could actually talk, if he wasn't stewing with rage over my actions.

The decision brought a pang of guilt into my chest, but I ignored it. I'd spent months shoving down that guilt before I'd confessed. I could live with it a little longer if it meant I could help Cade now.

"I'm going to break the hold they have over you," I said instead. "I've already—they tried to wipe my memories again, but I held onto them this time. We can fight this. *I'll* fight however I can for you."

"Oh, Trix." He crossed the last short distance between us and tugged me into a gentle embrace. My head bowed to his shoulder automatically, taking in his tart, coppery scent. He rumpled my hair in an affectionate gesture that took me back ten years in an instant. "Why am I not surprised? You're too good for them to keep you down. Too good for me, really."

The guilt jabbed right through my heart. Back home, no one other than Cade would have used the word "good" to describe me, not after years of me mouthing off at teachers and giving back crap at anyone who threw it at me. Even he shouldn't have thought that now.

"Not possible," I mumbled into his sweater. "And no way in hell are you a *bad* person. No one who isn't a psycho could blame you for getting that angry after everything with Sylvie."

"And the fact that you can say that shows just how much I don't deserve you," Cade teased. He pulled back just far enough to brush a quick peck to my forehead and then gazed down at me. Something shifted in his expression with a momentary narrowing of his eyes. "How did you know when to find me anyway? Elias told you? He's the only one who's talked to me at all since the... situation got this bad."

Out of all the other students, why only Elias? I'd have to ask the other guy that. "Well, it was Ryo who brought me out here the first time, when you were still... not yourself. He thought I deserved to know, after so long when no one had been willing to tell me anything. I don't think he realized you're still yourself any of the time. Elias told me what time to come out."

Cade nodded, but his gaze stayed intent. "They're looking out for you now, are they?"

My body resisted that representation, especially with my brother's arms still around me. "I wouldn't exactly say that. They've helped a little. It's not like I'd expect them to have my back the way you always have."

He made a humming sound. "No one could even really understand what we've shared. I know you'll stay on your toes. You know better than to trust the kind of assholes that end up at Roseborne."

Calling Ryo and Elias assholes hardly seemed fair—but then, Cade had been around them for months longer than I had, so he'd know things I wouldn't. It wasn't as if I'd planned on depending on them anyway.

"No point in trusting anyone except each other," I said, repeating the mantra that had become more true with each year we'd been together.

Cade smiled—and his stance went rigid. "Time's up," he said roughly, pulling away from me. "You'd better go. I don't like you seeing this." His shoulders twitched, a spasm running down his body.

My legs locked. How could I just run away from him? "If there's anything I can do that'll make it easier…?"

He shook his head. "You can't save me from this. No one should have to be around me when the monster takes over. It's fine. I've gotten used to the nights alone. You don't even need to—"

I cut him off before he could say anything more. "I'm coming back. Every night. You don't have to be alone anymore, I promise."

"Baby Bea," he said, in what could have been a thank you or a plea. His voice trailed off before he could take it in either direction. His back hunched, his limbs jerked at odd angles, and he let out a frustrated sound that could only be called a growl.

"I'll come back!" I said again, and forced myself to hurry away from him like he'd asked me to. My hands clenched at my sides as I strode back toward the school.

Roseborne's staff would pay for what they'd done to my brother. I didn't know how, but I wasn't going to back down until they had.

CHAPTER FIVE

Trix

$\mathcal{M}$ath class wasn't half as stressful now that I knew what to expect—and now that Elias wasn't going out of his way to avoid me like I had some kind of contagious deadly illness. He gave his lecture, some of my classmates made their attempts at working through the calculus question on the board, and like always, the figures shifted here and there of their own accord to completely throw us off.

It was annoying, but when you were prepared for it, not quite as unsettling as when I'd first noticed the weird changes. Elias still let out what looked like a restrained sigh at the end of class, looking at the string of calculations that, also as always, hadn't managed to reach an answer.

From what I'd gathered, these hopeless classes were part of his punishment. Not all of it, he'd indicated. I had no idea what else Roseborne was putting him through.

But while being set up as one of the teachers didn't give him any special exemptions in that area, I was hoping he had at least a little insight into his theoretical colleagues. When I brought my textbook up to his desk, I lingered there as the other students filed out.

"What can I do for you, Miss Corbyn?" he asked, with a glint in his dark eyes that turned his formal address into something more teasing.

He was in an okay mood, then, despite the frustrations of the class. I wouldn't mind getting to enjoy some of those higher spirits. I folded my arms loosely over my chest and gave him a wry smile in return. "I feel like I need a little extra instruction. Do you have time to go over a few things with me?"

"I'd be happy to see how I can assist." He glanced around, a shadow crossing his expression. "Maybe we could take the discussion outside? A change of scenery and fresh air can help keep your mind alert."

And also keep us farther from the prying senses of the regular staff. "Sounds good to me," I said.

He left a professional distance between us as we walked down the stairs and out onto the lawn. Elias didn't appear to be all that much older than me—mid-twenties, I'd guess from his looks—and while he was technically a teacher, he wasn't actually marking me or exerting any authority over my actions. I'd seen a glimmer of attraction in his gaze more than once when we were talking. Still, he seemed determined to stay restrained.

This time around, anyway. I had glimpses in my head of that chiseled face softened with laughter—and with something like adoration. Sometime in a past cycle, we'd gotten a hell of a lot more entangled than any real teacher and student should.

Now, he didn't speak until we'd made it halfway to the forest. "What's on your mind, Beatrix?"

Not as formal as using my last name, but definitely a way of putting up a bit of a wall between us. I decided not to hassle him about it, since I was about to ask him for a favor anyway.

"I mentioned yesterday that I wanted to get a better understanding of how the staff here operate," I said, lowering my voice. "I was thinking one way I could work toward that is by making myself a sort of teacher's pet to one of them, offering to help out and acting like I'm impressed by their methods... Maybe flattery will make them less cautious about what they let slip."

Elias nodded slowly. "I'm not sure how far you'll get taking that approach, but I can't see how it'd hurt either. Since I ended up here, I have seen students try to suck up for special treatment. You don't want to go overboard or they'll get suspicious, especially considering your history here, but they might like the idea that you're finally giving in. Whatever they are, I'd bet pride can still cloud their judgment."

Having his approval for the plan settled some of my nerves. Elias was definitely the most practical and focused of the three guys I'd found myself connecting with. Back in the world beyond Roseborne, he'd been building his own company from the ground up—and effectively.

"Do you have any idea which of the professors would be easiest to target?" I asked. "I mean, they all seem hostile toward us, but some of them definitely act more vindictive than others."

Elias tipped his head in thought, his mouth curving into a frown. "I'd avoid Marsden and Roth," he said after a moment. "They take too much enjoyment out of physically hurting us. Filch has always seemed very closed off to me... Ibbs has an outright vicious side if you rub her the wrong way... I'd probably go with Hubert or Carmichael, whichever you feel more comfortable talking to. They're more focused on emotional experiences, and I haven't seen them go out of their way to harm anyone otherwise."

I had Composition with Professor Hubert this afternoon—and while her approach to our writing assignments made my skin crawl, she had seemed more fascinated by our discomfort than vengeful. Professor Carmichael had left me with a chillier impression.

"All right," I said. "That helps a lot. Thank you."

The corner of Elias's mouth twitched upward. "I'm glad I can put my strategic thinking skills to some kind of use."

He should have been able to put them to all kinds of use. Looking over at him in his well-pressed suit with his commanding presence, I could easily picture him standing at the head of a boardroom, telling this person and that how to get their act together, laying out some inspired plan he'd been up half the night perfecting.

He glanced at me, catching me studying him, and the heat I'd noticed before flickered in his eyes. It sent an answering ripple through me. I suspected it was awfully enjoyable to have that commanding energy turned on you with the intent to please and pleasure, even if I couldn't remember much of my own past experiences with him.

With that thought came the memory of Cade's warning last night, his comment about the guys being assholes. Elias hadn't hidden his shame about his history. He'd admitted to me that he'd been cutthroat in his pursuit of success—that he'd stepped on people and shoved them aside to get what he wanted, and that one of those people had died because of his actions. Even if he regretted that now, I couldn't really know that those instincts wouldn't come out again if provoked.

And the memory brought up another question. I shifted my path so we'd skirt the woods rather than continuing into them and tipped my face to the thickly clouded sky. The faint sunlight that penetrated the gloom barely warmed my cheeks.

"Cade said you're the only one who's gone out to see him recently," I said. But it hadn't sounded as if my brother considered this guy a friend. "Why's that?"

Elias was silent for long enough that I started to think my question had offended him. Then he said, "I suppose it just happened that way. I go off on walks most nights to… to get away from the school. Our paths would cross. We didn't really talk much even when he was himself for more of the night, but sometimes I'd bring him leftovers from the kitchen." He paused. "I'm not sure I can say even that was totally selfless—it was something to distract myself with, something that made me feel I was doing things differently from before."

The things he'd done that had gotten him trapped here. I couldn't fault him for wanting to make a change from that.

Hearing him talk, another question I hadn't realized I'd want to ask itched at me. "Did you know the whole time, after I first came here, that he's the guy I was looking for?"

"I knew his name. It wasn't hard to figure out." Elias exhaled sharply. "You have to understand it's difficult to talk about the things that happen to us—ourselves or the other students—because of the way the powers here work. I couldn't have simply walked up to you and laid it out. And we all learn pretty quickly that it's easier not to get involved in anyone else's concerns. I did tell him that you'd come to the school."

"And he didn't want to see me."

"He didn't want *you* seeing him like that," Elias said. "I think he figured the staff would send you away eventually, and that you were more likely to go if you still weren't sure he was even on campus."

Which was true. Maybe I'd have done the same thing if our positions had been reversed. That didn't stop the sinking sensation in my gut, knowing Cade had been roaming around the woods for months aware of my presence here but never reaching out. Why hadn't he known that I cared about him enough that I'd keep searching until I found him, no matter what?

I'd show him how much he mattered to me. I'd make good on all the promises I'd given last night and then some.

"Thank you," I said to Elias again, my emotions too stirred up for me to want to take the conversation in another direction, and drifted back toward the school.

The one upside to restarting from scratch every time the staff felt I was becoming too much of a nuisance was that I got to skip a certain amount of work due to theoretically being a newbie. Composition class could be as harrowing as anything else the school threw at us, with Professor Hubert's constant encouragement that we "dig deep" into her themes that always touched on horrible moments from our pasts. From the reactions I'd seen when a student's offering disappointed her by sticking to less fraught ground, she punished those failures with a stomachache—or maybe worse.

During today's class, as she had everyone except me go up and share their tales of treasured objects that'd been broken, I eyed her as she watched each speaker. She really did light up to a sickening extent whenever any hint of anguish came into the student's expression or voice. You'd have thought she delighted in that misery.

Maybe she did.

Violet, who'd ended up in the same class as me for this iteration, went up to deliver her piece last, telling the story in her unexpectedly sweet voice of how she'd once dropped a piece of pottery she'd spent several art classes working on, and her classmates had done nothing but laugh while she'd swept up the shattered pieces. I might not have thought that attempting to blow them up was a proportionate response, but they did sound like jerks. The scarred girl kept her words steady, but her fingers gripped her notebook tight enough to crease the cover.

Hubert beamed at her when she'd finished. "Good, very good, Miss Droz. That wraps up our time here. Make sure you all bring open minds and willing pens to our next class."

I dawdled in picking up my purse and fitting my notebook into it, giving my classmates a chance to leave like I had in Math earlier. Then I ambled over to Professor Hubert's desk near the door. It took a concentrated effort to relax my grasp on my purse strap.

Sucking up to people wasn't really my strong point. Over the years, I'd learned to be a little more careful about saying exactly what I was thinking, but that was a far cry from actively buttering up a teacher who was probably psychotic and also not entirely human.

The professor glanced up at my approach. Her hand darted over the heap of cocoa-brown hair styled haphazardly on top of her narrow face. Her gaze turned piercing.

"This was a really interesting class," I said quickly, launching into the best spiel I could come up with before she could assume other intentions. "I've never seen a teacher get people thinking so much about their experiences. It seems like a great way to bring out our writing skills."

I didn't think Hubert cared about our actual skills at all, only about mining whatever angst she could, but she brightened a little even though her eyes stayed wary.

"I do try my best," she said. "You'll have the chance to experience the process yourself if you stick with us."

I let out an awkward laugh. "I'll admit I'm a little nervous about that, but I'm also kind of looking forward to seeing what comes out. Do you… have any tips for how to pick a topic that fits the theme and makes the most impact?"

Her expression was starting to relax. "Actually, I do. For the most part, it's about letting your emotions guide you rather than your thoughts. The logical side of you will want to avoid unpleasant recollections. If you can ignore that and simply sift through your memories to see what provokes the strongest response, that should guide you well."

"Ah." I widened my eyes as if struck by a revelation. "That's where people went wrong today, isn't it? Some of them talked about situations that hadn't affected them all that much, and then the stories fell flat."

"Exactly." Hubert looked downright pleased now. "It seems you have a good instinct for this sort of work already." Her fingers slid along her neck, fiddling with a gold chain I hadn't noticed before beneath the high collar of her blouse. A charm flashed at the V above the top button: a bird with its wings spread in flight. I only saw it for a second, and then she jerked her hand away, making it drop back out of sight.

"I guess I've always been interested in how our past

shapes who we end up becoming," I said, and decided I'd laid it on thick enough for one day. Time to slip in the offer I'd been leading up to and get out of here. "It'd be cool to see how you decide on the order of themes and that sort of thing—even the ones from before, so I'm not getting a sneak peek at what's coming up in class—if you ever have time for that. But I'll get out of your hair now."

"Well, I suppose we could see about that," Hubert said, and even gave me a slight wave as I stepped out of the classroom.

I resisted the urge to shake off the tension that had been building inside me. When I turned toward the staircase, I found that Violet had lingered near the banister. She was standing close enough to the classroom doorway that she'd probably heard that entire conversation.

She considered me with her hazel eyes: the one on the left surrounded by regular olive skin, the one of the right partly buried in the mess of half-healed burns. Her punishment for her crimes seemed to be that some of those wounds never totally healed. A couple of patches glared raw under the second-floor chandelier.

"What do you think you're doing, newbie?" she said, her melodic voice low enough to be almost menacing.

I stared right back at her, wondering how much I'd be screwing myself over if I let on how much I remembered, starkly aware of the power flowing through the rooms around us from its source two stories below.

"Is there some rule against talking to the professors?" I

asked. "It's not as if anyone else has been all that helpful since I got here."

"There's talking and then there's making a fool of yourself."

I caught myself before a totally snarky comment could slip out, although the one that did emerge might not have been that much wiser. "I don't know. I think what would be totally foolish is trying the same old thing over and over expecting to get a better result this time."

Her eyes twitched. Violet was pretty sharp—she'd probably caught the implication that I wasn't just talking about the two days I'd spent here so far.

Before she could push any harder, I strode past her and down the stairs. I could use some space to breathe while I waited to see if any of the seeds I'd planted in the last couple of days would grow into something real.

CHAPTER SIX

Ryo

The guy at the slick black table next to mine knifed over to vomit into his sink. The putrid smell of half-digested food and stomach acid rose up to join the horrible bouquet already emanating from the table in front of him, where another of our classmates was now simply clutching her belly with a pained expression. The girl in front of me was shaking with erratic spasms that had nearly knocked her off her stool.

And our Tolerance teacher, Professor Marsden, was watching this all with pursed lips and an approving gleam in her eyes.

The guy next to me tossed back the mixture of chemicals he'd been instructed to combine, his shoulders rigid. I was next in line after him—time to get started.

I sucked a breath through my mouth, which didn't do much to reduce the stink, and focused on the instruction sheet in front of me. After three years here at Roseborne, I'd gone through a full page of "observational exercises" and was now heading toward the end of the second set. This one involved three different test tubes of unknown liquids, a sugar-cube-like chunk of some grainy substance, and a packet of pale blue powder.

I poured the contents of the first tube into the second, dropped in the chunk and shook until it dissolved, added the third liquid, and finally dumped in the powder. As I swiveled the tube, the last addition turned the solution cloudy and a deeper blue.

My gut clenched despite myself. I glanced at the clock, kept swirling the mixture as the second hand ticked toward the top, and then gulped the stuff down.

Today's surprise burned down my throat and left a bitter aftertaste on my tongue. I didn't need to see the future to know this round would be an unpleasant one. Each stage was worse than the last.

Sweat was pouring off the forehead of the guy at my right now. He groaned with a choked hitch as if he could barely work the sound from his throat. His face was turning a purplish red. I braced myself, my stomach already starting to churn. The professor fluffed her black-and-white streaked curls.

"Don't forget to note down all your observations at the five-minute mark," she said in her sharply bright voice.

Or as close to the five-minute mark as we could manage amid the agony. I reached for my pencil anyway, as if holding onto it could ward off the worst of the potion's effects. Not for the first time, I thanked what gods there were that Trix hadn't ended up sharing this class with me yet. This was *not* how I ever wanted her to see me.

It wasn't so much the embarrassment of losing bodily control in itself. The thing I hated most about this class, even more than Archery where we literally let loose arrows at each other that I could attribute a few scars to, was how familiar it felt. The queasiness, the shakes, the frantic itching that some of the solutions provoked. The panicked impression that my innards would devour themselves. Now it was because of the substance I'd ingested. Before, the symptoms had risen up when I went too long without replenishing my high with my drug of choice.

I'd been through a full withdrawal during my first few weeks here. These sessions just extended that experience, sending me back over and over to the pains of that awful stretch of time and the similar, if shorter, horrible moments that had come before it back home.

Despite the number of ingredients, the impact of today's offering was relatively simple. A burning ache split through the queasiness in my stomach. I only had a fraction of a second to register the shift inside me before I was throwing myself toward the sink, spewing a soupy-sour mess into the stainless steel basin. With each involuntary retch, the ache inside seared sharper and deeper, like someone was slicing me open with a razor blade while I puked.

Dizziness swam over my mind. I nearly slipped off my stool. My gut was still heaving, though, a thin dribble of spittle emerging from my exhausted throat. I held there, only half on my seat, clutching the faucet until I was sure I'd expelled everything that was going to come out.

The hiss of the water was almost soothing. I rinsed the sink automatically, scooped up a little water to wash out my mouth as well as I could, and settled back onto my stool. The razor was still carving its way through my abdomen. The dizziness had shifted into a splinter of a headache right through the center of my forehead. I closed my eyes for a second, found that only amplified the pain, and forced myself to retrieve the pencil that had rolled across the table when I'd dropped it.

Did anyone bother to read the notes we jotted down about how sick we'd felt, even Marsden? I was pretty sure the point wasn't for the professors to evaluate our experiences but to make us relive them a second time, dwelling on the exact awfulness of the sensations so we could describe them accurately. Twice the torture for the same effort.

Being one of the oldest students here meant I took my turn toward the end. It was only ten minutes later that Marsden waved for us to leave, and my stomach was still aching and my head throbbing mildly. And lucky me, I had a counseling session in a few hours... after lunch, which at this moment I had even less interest in than usual.

Even in the middle of my discomfort, I couldn't stop my eyes from automatically scanning the second-floor hall to see if Trix happened to be around. The pleasure of her company wouldn't wipe away the pain, but at least talking with her would distract me from it.

No such luck. I stopped to lean against the railing overlooking the staircase, peering down there just in case, and one of my Tolerance classmates came up beside me.

"Still hung up on our valiant white knight, Shibata?" he said with an unrestrained sneer.

I didn't think the guy was more than eighteen, probably plucked straight out of high school. I couldn't remember his name—Andy? Zander? Something like that. He couldn't have been around for more than a few months before Trix had made her first arrival, but apparently he thought that gave him enough seniority to take deep offense to her presence.

Most caustic people could be diffused if you simply didn't care enough to give them a real reaction. I offered a half-hearted shrug. "What's it to you who I hang out with?"

He snorted. "It's pathetic, that's all. She's off in her delusional loop thinking she's going to save this brother of hers and whoever else here, and you go trotting after her like a sad little puppy every time."

With an attitude like that, it wasn't hard to figure out how he might have ended up at Roseborne. He was obviously still in the blame-everyone-around-me stage of recognizing his failings.

"If you don't like watching, there are plenty of other places to look," I said mildly, and ambled off before he could berate me any more.

A lot of the jerks who ended up here were bullies in one way or another. They'd gotten off on making people feel small in the real world, and they tried to set up the same dynamic at the college. From what I'd seen, that was the type who sputtered out of existence the soonest.

Roseborne punished defiance and rewarded penitence. Nothing you did would grant you a free pass, but if you could recognize how you'd gotten yourself into this mess, you at least got a bit more time to appreciate the few enjoyable shards left in this charade of an existence.

Thankfully, by the time lunch hour rolled around, the effects of Tolerance class had completely faded away. I plowed through the alternately wilted and stringy chicken Caesar salad with as little attention to my taste buds as I could manage and then fiddled with the cheap fork until I'd managed to twist it into the figure of a snail. Trix might like that. I slipped it into my pocket as I headed out. If she'd ducked in to grab some food, she'd left again so quickly I hadn't seen her.

Not that we'd have had much time together anyway. I turned my reluctant feet toward the counseling room.

What reminder would I get today of what a fuckup I'd been? You could never know for sure, only that whatever the room showed you, it was pretty much guaranteed to get under your skin. I waited in the hall for a few minutes until the door swung open and a guy walked out with his shoulders hunched and his face wan. The session hadn't gone easy on him.

I took a deep breath and stepped into the small white room. As usual, it was empty other than the plain wooden chair in the center of the room. I flopped down into it and braced myself for the show to start.

The images swam into focus across the walls slowly,

wavering back and forth. It took a moment before I recognized my parents' bedroom back home. The walls of the counseling room split between different angles with erratic jerks: groping under the bed, pawing through the closet, yanking open drawer after drawer on the maple dresser. My stomach twisted with a nausea that nothing I drank in Tolerance could ever compete with.

"Where is it?" a voice muttered as if from all around me. My voice, ragged with desperation. "There's got to be something. Come on, come on."

The images spun, and suddenly my parents were looming over me—in the kitchen, with more sunlight than I'd seen in years streaming through the broad windows behind them. I couldn't take any pleasure in that when their expressions were so pained. My mother had lowered her head, her fingers tangled in her amber-brown waves as she let out soft little sobs. My father's mouth was pressed flat. He ran his hand over his face and into the smooth black hair I'd inherited from him.

"My grandmother brought that jewelry box with her from Kyoto. All she wanted was for it to stay in the family. How could you not even *think* about the rest of us?"

My hands shifted in my lap of their own accord, remembering the intricate details of the carved wood, the delicate lines of paint. Sold to a pawnshop for no more than a tenth of what it'd probably been worth, and that wasn't even including the personal significance.

My great-grandmother had died just a year before I'd pawned off her heirloom. I *hadn't* been thinking, not really, not about anything but getting the fix I was dying for—and, if I'd been capable of admitting it back then, dying because of.

I'll get it back, I wanted to tell him. Maybe I had even told him that in the moment—I couldn't remember. Chances were I'd either been high or jonesing to get there. By that point, the spaces in between those states had gotten awfully short.

It'd be gone now anyway. That'd been almost four years ago. Four fucking years.

"We just want to help you, Ryo," my mother said in a rasp that spoke of held-back tears. "We just want you back the way you were. If you'd just let us—"

"If you want to help me, then leave me the fuck alone!" nineteen-year-old me shouted back, and swiped a plate off the counter so it shattered on the floor for effect, just because I could. Because the last thing I'd wanted to hear was their concern when everything I did just cut them deeper.

The walls blinked into another moment, I couldn't have said how many months later. A punch thrown at my father's face; a jet of red blood streaming from his nose. My mother's weeping carrying from behind their closed bedroom door.

Blink. My little brother was staring at me shocked and betrayed as I clutched the video game system he'd saved up for in my hands. "What are you *doing*, Ryo?"

I closed my eyes and covered them for good measure. The sounds just got louder, penetrating straight through my brain.

This was my penitence. This was what I deserved. To

own up to what a shitty excuse for a human being I'd been, over and over and over again. No matter how much I accepted it, no matter how many confessions I made in Composition or potions I drank in Tolerance, I'd never really make up for it.

All I could do that mattered even a little was lift Trix up rather than drag her down like I had so many of the other people I'd loved.

CHAPTER SEVEN

Trix

The pickings in the kitchen were pretty slim, but I managed to roll up some sliced ham and a few not-too-wilted pieces of lettuce in a pita to make a passable wrap. Elias's comment about bringing Cade food had stuck with me.

I hadn't let myself think about how he was sustaining himself out there in the forest. With the monstrous teeth and jaws he had most of the time now, I guessed he hunted down meals like any animal predator would. How could that do anything but make him feel less human by the day?

The staff apparently didn't care if we poked around in the kitchen after hours. No one showed up to question my presence there. I guessed they'd never hassled Elias either, or he'd have mentioned that.

I found a produce bag to hold the offering and tucked

that into my purse. Then I headed out into the night.

The first time I'd gone wandering into the woods by moonlight, before I'd known Cade was living out there, the shifting shadows and the eerie quiet had stirred up memories not from my times on campus but from my life before that. Uneasy memories. The times I'd ventured into the forest since then, I'd been so focused on my purpose that either there hadn't been room in my head for those fragments to rise up or I simply hadn't noticed them.

Now, as I walked toward the area where I'd found Cade before, pieces of that past jostled loose to join the anxious questions about the present that were already swimming through my mind. In the creak of a branch, I heard a foster mother's footsteps on the basement stairs, coming down to drag me out of bed and yell at me about whatever she thought I'd done wrong this time. The faint brush of the breeze over my skin brought back the leering gaze of my first foster father. The hoarse call of a distant bird reminded me of the Monroes' raucous laughter at the thought that I'd ever make anything useful of myself.

I didn't want to think about any of those times, any of those people. I'd gotten through all the shit the families I'd been placed with—and the one I'd been born into—had thrown at me, partly with Cade's help. Dwelling on it didn't help anyone, least of all him.

But that was how the whole school operated, wasn't it? Every class, every assignment, designed to draw out the worst parts of your history. Maybe I should be glad that most of the material Roseborne had to work with cast me as the victim, because remembering times when I'd hurt someone else would have felt even worse.

Even as that thought passed through my head, my phone's light glanced off a mica-laced rock. The sparkle hit my eyes like the glint of broken glass, and my lungs seized up. I inhaled sharply and shoved that memory away as hard as I could.

Focus on finding Cade. Focus on figuring out how to break the spell this place had cast over him and everyone else. That was the best atonement I could offer.

The sense of being chased by my past had made me walk faster. I reached the heart of the woods a little before the half hour. I hesitated in the same small patch of open ground—so small that calling it a clearing would have seemed ridiculous—and looked around.

Would Cade even be human yet? How would he react to me while he was in his monstrous form? The first time I'd seen him, when Ryo had brought me out here, he'd sprang at me, knocked me down and pinned me with those heavy paws. Now, maybe he'd have a more concrete understanding of who I was and that I was really here. Or maybe whatever he'd heard of my confession would bring out more aggressive urges than before. He didn't want me around him when he wasn't himself—that much he'd made incredibly clear.

He used to get like that sometimes when I'd witnessed him laying into one friend or another who'd pissed him off, when the harshness of his words during that moment had been enough to leave me briefly unsteady around him in the aftermath. Of course he'd noticed. *You don't want to be around someone like me,* he'd say, turning away from me. *It's okay—you don't have to pretend.*

That had always been enough to shake me out of my discomfort. I knew the real him, after all. I'd assure him over and over that I loved him all the same, and he'd come back and tuck me close. *I guess it takes one screw-up to really care about another, huh?*

But this—the creature he became, the awful magic that bound him so tightly... It was a hell of a lot more than a quick outburst of temper. It wasn't him at all, but something Roseborne had inflicted on him. I didn't know what I could say that would convince him it was okay with me, because it *wasn't*, even if that wasn't his fault.

I stayed in place, picking at a loose thread on my purse strap, until the clock reached twelve thirty. "Cade?" I called out. I had told him I'd come back. He'd have believed that, wouldn't he, however much comfort the promise had given him?

Almost immediately, the sound of footsteps reached my ears. My brother moved through the trees to meet me, his stride more purposeful than it'd been the last two times. More sure of what he could expect from me. Good. I wanted him to know he could count on me now, even if I'd screwed so much up before.

"Trix," he said, his crooked grin softened by relief, and I couldn't stop the smile that sprang to my face in return, even though there wasn't much to smile about in this awful situation.

"I told you I'd come," I said, and fished the wrap out of my purse. "And I brought you something to eat. Elias said he's done that sometimes. I'm sorry I didn't think of it before."

Cade's expression flickered at the mention of his previous benefactor, but the hint of emotion left his face so quickly I couldn't tell how he actually felt. He took the food from me eagerly enough and dug into the pita with an enthusiastic bite.

I wasn't going to ask him about his usual eating habits, but the subject I was planning on bringing up wasn't exactly a fun one either. I grappled with the words for several seconds while he ate before deciding on the right ones.

"I'm trying to understand how everything works here so that I can figure out ways to disrupt that. One of the things I keep wondering about is how the school or the staff here pick new students to begin with. We were living two states away. How did they even know you exist?"

Cade paused halfway through the wrap with a frown. "I don't know. They've never explained—that's not the kind of question they'd want to answer. No one I talked to back when I still hung out at the school seemed to be sure either."

"Do you remember anything strange or just different that happened in the week or two before you got the scholarship letter?"

If thinking back to that time—to the freedom he'd had and the violence he'd succumbed to within that freedom— bothered him, he didn't show it. He took another bite and chewed thoughtfully. "Definitely nothing outright strange. I'd remember that. The only thing I can think of that changed around then was there was a new girl who came around to a couple of get-togethers with a bunch of my friends. I don't know if you met her." He paused, and his gray eyes darkened. "I hardly talked to her, but I think she was there when I caught Richie saying shit about Sylvie."

Which was the reason he'd assumed Richie had been behind the prankish accident that had led to her death. The reason he'd wailed on him the way he had. My stomach knotted. "Did you get into a fight with him there?"

"I gave him hell, and there might have been a little scuffle. I wasn't really sure until I looked through what he'd been posting online and all that afterward."

But he'd been wrong in that certainty. The impulse to remind him of that caught in my throat.

A new girl in Cade's friend group wasn't that unusual anyway. His guy friends brought around new girlfriends and chicks they were hoping to turn into girlfriends or at least one-night-stands pretty regularly. Maybe she'd been connected to Roseborne somehow—or maybe he'd been identified by a random observer, or a clue in an article about the beating, or a gazillion other things that might have been enough for a supernatural being to connect the dots.

Cade polished off the rest of the wrap while I thought the possibilities over. He swiped at his mouth. "Sometimes you've just got to put people in their place," he said. "Show them they can't actually get away with their shit. You remember that asshole sophomore—what was his name? Clement?"

My spine stiffened automatically. "Yeah." Clement— the prick who'd ended up in half of my tenth grade classes, who'd started cornering me every moment he managed to catch me alone to tell me all the filthy things he wanted to do to me. Punching him in the jaw hadn't been enough to get him to back off. The next time he'd gone straight for a grope. Unluckily for him, Cade had happened to catch that moment.

"Suspended for a week," Cade said in a nostalgic tone, rolling his shoulders. "But it was worth it seeing him need crutches for six times longer than that. He wasn't chasing after any girls for a while." He caught my gaze, his abruptly intent. "I'd do it again for you a dozen times over if I had to. No one messes with what's mine."

His sister. His best friend. His confidant. Hearing him call me "his" had always lit a reassuring spark of warmth in my chest.

At least, almost always. In that moment, I couldn't help thinking of afterward, when he'd found me in my bedroom, touched me with his raw-knuckled hands and said, "You're mine, aren't you? Show me how much you're mine, Baby Bea." And even though the turmoil in his expression had unnerved me—or maybe partly because it had—I'd opened up to him in every way I could. If he needed to be that close to me to be sure of me, then who was I to say no?

Now, Cade stepped toward me and raised his hand to my cheek, the backs of his fingers just barely grazing my skin. My pulse hiccupped with the conflicting desires to recoil and to lean into him and accept whatever tenderness he'd offer.

Was he mine too, really? What did I even want that to mean? The bond between us had become so tangled over the years I wasn't really sure how to tell. He was my brother... but somehow things were much more complicated now.

I didn't have to decide in that exact moment. A shudder ran through Cade's body. He pulled back, his wiry muscles tensing beneath his clothes, and I knew before he said anything that the change was coming over him.

"I'll leave," I said, so he didn't have to tell me to. "But I'll be back again tomorrow. If you need anything—"

He shook his head, his mouth twisting. "Just go. I'll— I'll see if I can think of anything else."

My legs locked for a second, every instinct telling me I *shouldn't* leave someone I cared about when he was in distress, but the flash of his eyes as he waved me off thawed my resistance.

I should ask Ryo and the others what they'd noticed around the time they'd gotten their scholarship offers, I thought as I hurried back through the woods. If they could even tell me. I'd known how to ask Cade because it'd been easy to see what incident must have grabbed the school's attention. I didn't know any specifics about what had brought the three guys who'd become my allies—and at times my lovers—here.

That would have to wait until at least the morning,

though. In the meantime, I had one other plan for tonight.

As soon as I'd slipped into the school building, I darted upstairs to the second floor and went to the art room. Somewhere in the last transition, I'd lost the reward card I'd been using to jimmy the locks, but I had a gift card I might never get to use that would serve the same purpose no problem. I eased it into the narrow gap by the frame and pressed it against the latch.

With a push and a twist of the knob at the same time, the lock popped open. I hustled inside. Who knew how much time I had before the staff caught on to my breaking and entering?

Where would Professor Filch keep his reference photos? I checked each drawer on the teacher's desk, my heart thumping faster by the second, and then turned to the filing cabinet in the corner with its sprinkling of rust. Those drawers proved to be locked, but I'd learned a trick for that too that might work. Hefting the unit backward with a faint rattle of the shifting contents, I felt underneath it for the bar that would release the bolts above.

There. They clicked, and the drawers slid open at my tug. I riffled through the folders as quickly as I could. At the back of the top drawer, I caught a glimpse of faded sepia photopaper.

I tugged out that folder and opened it on the desk under the light of my phone. The pictures weren't totally sepia-toned. The backgrounds had that faded yellow quality, but a sheen of color marked the faces, hair, and clothes of the eight student portraits inside.

I couldn't spend the night in here analyzing them. With a flick of my thumb, I brought up my phone's camera and snapped a picture of each photograph. I'd just gotten to the second from the last when my hand hesitated over them.

The seventh photograph showed a girl who looked, on close inspection, to be maybe seventeen or eighteen, just a tad younger than me. Her dark hair hung loose to her shoulders and her chin was raised at an angle that looked almost hostile, but that wasn't what had caught my attention. No, it was the chain with its hint of gold around her neck, the edge of a charm just visible at the collar of her shirt. An edge that looked like the tip of a bird's wing.

Like the necklace Professor Hubert kept tucked inside her own blouse.

Had she or someone else stolen it from this girl? Was it tied to her power somehow? I squinted at the picture in the tiny pool of artificial light, and an eerie impression crept over my skin.

The girl's hair was styled very differently from Professor Hubert's, and it wasn't quite as dark a brown. I didn't think her eyes were the same shade, and the shape of her face was softer. But her gaze had a piercing quality that felt familiar in a way that ran through me down to my bones.

She couldn't be the same person, right? From the look of the photographs, they'd been taken several decades ago, and I'd have placed Hubert in her forties. I never would have noticed any resemblance at all if the necklace hadn't caught my eye.

But then, who could say what was plausible when supernatural powers were in the mix? This girl could have been a long-ago relative... or some strange magic could have carried her across the years and reshaped her features.

A faint groan emanated through the building. My body went rigid where I stood. It might not be anything other than the foundation shifting, but I shouldn't have lingered here as long as I had. Any second one of the professors would burst in and catch me.

I snapped pictures of the last two photographs as quickly as I could, shoved them all back into their folder, and wiggled that into its spot at the back of the filing cabinet. Tucking my phone into my purse, I slunk to the door.

No sound carried from outside. I'd been in here at least fifteen minutes. During my last cycle, the dean had caught me in his office in less than ten. Professor Marsden had interrupted Jenson playing one of the music room instruments in no more than two. Surely one of them would have noticed I'd disturbed the school's security by now. Was someone waiting out there to catch me in the act?

I waited too. As the minutes slipped by, a growing tickle of excitement expanded through my chest. No one came.

I eased open the door and found the hall on the other

side empty. As far as I could tell, no one was stirring in the whole school.

As I crept down the hall to the dorms, the tickle rose higher, tinged with anticipation now. I'd managed to shake the staff's power to wipe my memories this time around. What if I'd managed to escape more of their magic than that? By all appearances, they could no longer detect when I snuck into places I wasn't meant to be.

Imagine all the things I could do under their noses now.

CHAPTER EIGHT

Trix

"Do they have what you're looking for in here?" Ryo asked.

"I'm not sure yet." I dug through one of the toolboxes on the shelving unit in the maintenance shed off the side of the school. We'd already poked around through the equipment in the carriage house but hadn't turned up anything I thought I could use in there. "If I'm out of luck, I guess I'll make do with a knife from the kitchen or something." There was an axe leaning against the wall near the cot, but that was probably too big and unwieldy for this specific purpose.

A whiff of dust wafted up from the toolbox. I couldn't restrain a sneeze. Ryo grinned from where he was standing by the door, which we'd left ajar so he could keep watch for any staff or students I didn't trust coming this way.

"Obviously you're the first person to bother trying to fix anything around here in a long time. Well, if you can call carving a hole in a wall 'fixing.'"

"If I carve it right, I'll fix a whole lot of things," I muttered, moving to the next shelf.

I hadn't slept much last night, my mind spinning with the possibilities of being able to take covert action without the staff catching on. The one thing that was clear to me was that the school's power was tied to that underground rosebush. If I could cut off the source, then no one should be able to stop us from leaving. I could hope the curses that gripped all the students would fade too.

But to get to that twisted plant, to figure out the best way to tackle it, I had to get back into the secret basement area. As far as I knew, it had only one entrance, and that was secured by a heavy padlock. I'd only managed to break through the door before in a hasty, desperate maneuver involving one of the shields from the suits of armor—a maneuver I couldn't replicate, even if I'd thought I could manage that without alerting the staff just from the clatter it'd make, now that they'd removed those shields.

So far neither I nor the guys had come closer to getting our hands on the key to that padlock. I wasn't willing to wait around assuming that we eventually would. But if I could have enough time to myself undetected, there was another option.

The secret basement stood next to the regular basement we students had access to for laundry duty and other chores. All that stood between one and the other was a single concrete wall. If I could chip away a passage just large enough for me to squeeze through without it being discovered, I'd have access to the staff's creepy base of operations.

How thick could that wall be? A foot? Two at most? If I could just get my hands on a halfway decent—

"Ah ha!" My hand closed around the handle of a sturdy-looking chisel, the whole tool solid metal and almost as long as my forearm. A speckling of rust colored the surface, but nothing serious. I brandished it for Ryo's approval. "Now we're talking."

I'd already tucked the hammer I'd found into my purse. I set the chisel in with it. The end poked out, but I could cover that with my arm.

Ryo gave me a light clap, still grinning. "It certainly doesn't look like anyone will notice they're missing."

"Nope. The trick now is going to be finding a spot to tackle the wall where people won't notice the hole." I wasn't optimistic enough to think I'd pull the whole scheme off in a single night.

"Sounds like you've got it all figured out."

I let out a rough laugh. "I wish I felt like I did." The doubts that I'd been grappling with along with my plans surged up. "What if I do get caught, and they manage to wipe my mind this time, and I lose even that advantage? What if I pull this off, and everyone's just stuck the way they are now instead of it helping them?" I might condemn Cade to a lifetime as a monster if I handled this wrong.

Ryo stepped up to me and tucked his arm around my waist. "You've got this, Trix," he said in that gentle, mellow way of his. "The fact that you've already managed to pull this much over on the staff is amazing. I'm honored just to be here watching."

I rolled my eyes at the effusive praise, but at the same time I couldn't help smiling. I'd admitted those doubts to Ryo because I'd known he'd reassure me, hadn't I?

The thought brought a weird wave of emotion with it, guilt and uncertainty rising up under the relief. Who was I to go looking for comfort when I *owed* it to at least one person here to make things right because of what I'd done? Ryo didn't know the worst parts of me—he couldn't know more than fragments of my history. I could feel that I'd never let myself reveal more than that.

And who was *he*, really? Cade had warned me against him. I didn't know what had brought him here or what curse he was operating under. Maybe I hadn't wanted to know because it was so much easier to survive here when I had someone I could turn to, but that was the kind of thinking that got you screwed over.

"Can I ask you something?" I said.

"Can I stop you?" Ryo teased, but a shadow crossed his face as if he suspected where this conversation might go.

I had to phrase the question right so that he could answer it. It'd become clear during my time on campus that Roseborne's students couldn't outright say what they believed they'd been brought here for or how they were being punished for those actions. But more general questions about their past were fair game, even if those ended up leading to the same answers.

I let my hand come to rest on Ryo's arm as I spoke, where I'd be able to feel his response in his body as well as watch it. "You've hinted before that you've got a lot on your conscience. What was so bad about your life before you came here?" *What awful thing did* you *do?*

The muscles in his arm tensed as I'd thought they might, but he kept holding my gaze. "You don't remember any of that? We talked about it once, at least some of it—but it was a while ago."

I shook my head. "Everything before the last time is still pretty sketchy."

"Well..." He dragged in a breath and exhaled slowly. "If you want to know, then you should. I wasn't trying to hide it, I just... don't like talking about it. I can't even tell you how ashamed I am when I think back to those last few years, not that feeling bad about it makes up for anything.

"It's a pretty mundane story, really. In high school I was bored and started hanging out with some friends who were into various recreational substances. The drugs added a little spark when things were dull. But I tried harder and harder stuff, and ended up hooked—meth is fucking brutal. It turns you into a vicious, heartless person."

As he spoke, my own stance had stiffened. Ryo let his hand slip from my back as if he were afraid I'd resent the contact. He looked away for a second before meeting my eyes again. "I stole all kinds of things from my family. I said horrible things to them I can never take back. I destroyed every real friendship I had, sometimes over and over, in more ways than one. I—"

I tightened my grip on his arm, and he stopped with a questioning expression, braced as if prepared for me to berate him for his sins.

My throat had closed up. I had to swallow hard before I could speak. "I know what that looks like. My birth parents—I don't remember a lot from back then, because I got taken into foster care when I was five, but I know the drugs meant more to them than I ever did."

Ryo's eyes widened. "Shit. I didn't know—you didn't tell me that before."

I guessed I'd never been comfortable sharing that much when it'd seemed I'd only known him for a matter of days rather than the months I knew it was now. I hesitated over my next words. "I've had friends who got caught up in that kind of life too. It's not— It's awful to watch and awful to be around. I'm glad I didn't know you then. But you've obviously found a way to be more than an addict too, and that matters."

It wasn't like me. I'd hurt someone with nothing more than my own emotions and selfishness screwing with my head.

For a second, Ryo didn't speak, only gazed down at me as if he didn't know what to make of that statement. Then he leaned in and kissed me, quick but hard. He left his head bowed next to mine afterward.

"I'm trying," he said, the hoarseness in his voice deepening. "Meeting you helped me see that I could do something that mattered for someone else, even here… even if I haven't gone about it in the best ways all the time."

My gut twisted. If he realized how messed up *I* was…

Even the person who'd cared about me the most hadn't been able to stand keeping me this close for very long.

I forced myself to put on another smile as I eased back. "I'm not going to complain. Compared to how everyone else here has treated me, you've been a saint." I hefted my purse, much heavier now with the tools in it. "But I'd better get on with my mission before anyone wonders why we've been hanging out in here so long."

Ryo searched my face as if he suspected there was more to my abrupt shift in topic than I was letting on, but he didn't push. He never did, did he? He was just *there*, waiting for me to open up in my own time. Trusting that whatever I offered him then would be worth it.

We parted ways as we came into the school. I headed straight down to the basement on the left-hand side to consider my options, a perfect excuse to bury the emotions prickling inside me even deeper.

The basement hall the students had access to was short, just a few rooms branching off from it. The laundry room at the bottom of the stairs stood to the right—the same direction as where the staff's secret basement lay. No one was using the ancient machines in there right now. I wandered in and scanned the room.

The far wall would be the one I needed to chisel my

way through. A row of three industrial-sized dryers stood along it. That might be just what I needed. I crouched down in the musty-smelling space beside one, set the tools out of view behind it, and then gave the machine a testing heave.

When I put my back into it, I could shift it a couple of inches at a time. Perfect. When there was less chance of being interrupted, I'd sneak down here, move the dryer far enough out to squeeze behind it, and chip away at the concrete where no one would see the growing hole once I'd shoved it back into place.

Listening carefully for anyone coming down the stairs, I pushed the machine back and slid my tools right under it so they'd be totally out of sight. It'd be safer leaving them here than constantly secreting them to and from my dorm.

As I straightened up, footsteps rasped against the steps. I brushed myself off and hurried out of the laundry room, an excuse ready on my tongue. Easy enough to say I couldn't find some piece of clothing and had come down to see if it'd been left in one of the machines.

The footsteps belonged to Jenson, ducking his head instinctively as he came out of the stairwell into the hall, although the ceiling was a good foot over his considerable height. My stance relaxed some, if not completely. It was still hard to be sure of exactly where I stood with him.

He raised his eyebrows as he glanced at me and then the space around me. "What are you up to down here, Trixie?"

The nickname brought back a tickle of memory—of him using it sometime in the past, me swatting him in annoyance. I still didn't like it, but it was hard to be too irritated with the playful affection in his voice.

"It's Trix," I corrected without much rancor. "Are you following me around or something now?"

He waved a hand dismissively. "Will you believe that I was just in the cafeteria and thought I saw you heading this way?"

He had to make it a question to give a somewhat straight answer. I let out my breath in a huff. "Okay. But I think it's better if you're not involved in any plans I've got down here." The staff might not be able to pick up on *my* odd activities, but they should still be able to sense if *he* went somewhere they wouldn't expect him to be.

"You're set on being the lone wolf, huh?" he said with a lift of his eyebrows.

"Some things I've got to do on my own if I want to be sure they'll actually get done," I replied.

I regretted the off-the-cuff response in an instant at the tightening of his expression. He recovered almost immediately with a casual shrug, but my dismissal must have hurt him more than I'd have expected it to.

Why wouldn't it have? He was extending a hand the only way he could, and I'd basically smacked it away. After laying into him for giving me a hard time before, I was brushing off his attempts to do the opposite.

"I didn't mean—it's more about this place than it is about how I think about you," I said quickly.

"Don't worry about my ego," Jenson said in his careless way. "I'm made of steel—impervious."

I'd have known that was a lie even if I hadn't been

aware of his situation. Something about the claim and the way his bright blue eyes lingered on me brought me back to that moment just a few days ago when he'd sung his heart out in the music room for me. Almost literally— from the way he'd toppled when the professors had caught him, they might as well have been crushing his chest.

Every statement he said to me might be a lie, but the things he'd done hadn't been. The things he'd done for me. What the hell had *I* done in those times I only recalled slivers of to earn that kind of devotion—from not just him but Ryo and to some extent Elias too?

How selfish was I that I wanted to indulge in all of it?

But maybe it wasn't selfish if a little indulgence let me show my appreciation and cover the tracks of my larger plan at the same time. If it was weird to want three guys at once, who the fuck cared? It'd be about the least weird thing about this psychotic place.

I held out my hand, ignoring the uncertain thump of my pulse. "You *could* give me an excuse for why I've been down here."

"How can I refuse an offer like that?" Jenson said, a pleased gleam coming into his eyes. He took my hand and let me tug him into the laundry room.

I leaned against the folding table and pulled him into a kiss. Jenson met me with equal enthusiasm. There were no lies in the way his mouth caught mine, in the heat that formed between our bodies, in the caress of his hand down my side. When I let my teeth graze his lower lip teasingly, he let out a hum that was almost a groan and gripped my waist to tug me even closer.

I didn't intend to take the encounter much farther than this. Not far enough that it'd seem like a promise rather than just fooling around. But for a few very enjoyable moments, I managed to convince myself a little making out was all for the greater good.

CHAPTER NINE

Elias

I couldn't say I ever felt all that comfortable in Roseborne's cafeteria, especially now that I wasn't required to attend most of the school's classes. The majority of the students currently in residence had much more experience with me as their math teacher than as a classmate. Even the guys I shared my dorm bedroom with got a little quieter when I was around.

None of them matter one bit, my grandfather would have said. *You move forward and make your name for yourself, and let the weaklings grouse all they want behind your back. Soon enough they'll be fawning to your face to try to benefit from your success.*

Not much chance of that here. What was I going to be successful at—teaching the most pointless class in existence? Surviving long enough to see everyone who'd been here when I arrived on campus waste away?

Negative thinking is the loser's route.

Right. How would Grandpa DeLeon have handled this place, I'd like to know.

In the moment, all I could do was eat as quickly as possible at the corner of the table I'd picked out, staying out of everyone else's way so they wouldn't feel the need to clam up. It wasn't as if our dinner offered much to relish anyway.

Maybe I could have gone to Trix for company, if that wouldn't paint an even larger target on her. But when I'd come in, she'd already been sitting at a full table with Ryo beside her, naturally. The guy might not put a whole lot of effort into his own life, but he seemed determined to be as much a part of Trix's as he could manage.

Why are you letting him? asked my grandfather's voice in my head. *Who is he that she'd want to spend her time with him and not you? Act like the DeLeon you are and show her how much better she could have it—or forget about her and focus on more important things.*

What could be more important? I wanted to demand of him. *She could be our key to getting out of this place.* She'd already been the key to my starting to accept just how deeply my grandfather had warped my perspective. He wouldn't have appreciated that development, though.

As I picked through the last of my boiled vegetables, Trix and Ryo got up together. Walking to the front table where we left our dirty dishes, Ryo made a comment that brought a smile to Trix's lips. They set down their plates, and he rested his hand on the small of her back as they headed out. An affectionate gesture, sure, but also one you could see as possessive.

Why *should* he take the leading role here? I could offer her a hell of a lot more than just about anyone in this school. My fingers tightened around my fork. As soon as I'd eaten, I'd find them and step in, and—

I caught myself with a grimace. What was I really going to offer her while we were trapped in here? Nothing I'd built out in the real world mattered now. Frankly, a lot of it hadn't mattered even at the time. All the deals and awards had been just one more way to puff myself up, to prove to my grandfather I was following in his footsteps, that he'd been right to invest as much as he had in me.

Building and building and not caring who around me got crushed under the weight of those plans.

That time when Trix and I had ended up connecting, when we'd gotten so close that my chest ached with the memory—how much had I offered her then? Could I honestly say I'd given her more than she'd given me?

I could change that, though. I wanted her—I wanted to be the man she'd pick if it came to the point when she needed to. No, I wanted her to pick me even *if* there wasn't any need to narrow down her options. If we ever got out of here, I didn't intend to just walk away.

She'd talked about cozying up to the professors. I'd already planned on trying out that tactic myself. After all, I acted like part of the teaching staff most of the time. Seeing Ryo hovering over her only made me more determined.

Trix needed to know she wasn't alone in this quest—

and that I could do more than talk about how much I supported her.

Dean Wainhouse kept office hours for a little while after dinner most weekdays. After I'd gulped down the last of my dinner, I strode down the hall to his door. I didn't feel as though I wielded any real influence within the school, but people tended to have more confidence in you if you showed confidence in yourself.

The dean answered my knock with a somewhat weary look that wasn't promising. "Mr. DeLeon. What can I do for you?"

I forged ahead as if I had no reason to doubt how my suggestion would be received. "I was hoping to discuss my role in the school and how I might expand on it, to everyone's benefit."

His gaze sharpened slightly, skimming over me in evaluation. "Why don't you come in and tell me what you're thinking, then?"

It'd been a while since I was last in the dean's office, but the room had a vibe that'd been familiar from the very first time: the unmistakable but undeniable whiff of long-standing authority. He might as well have been a CEO over a century-old company as the dictator over this college.

Traditionally-minded leaders could be budged. You just had to find the right angle. They needed respect, even adulation—as far as they were concerned, the best judge of a person's character was whether that person recognized the leader's worth.

I stationed myself in front of the dean's desk with my

hands folded in front of me and a deferential dip of my head that I didn't let irk me. "In the last year or so, since my focus has been on teaching my own class, I've had a lot of time to observe the overall running of the college. And I have to say I've been impressed. The discipline you exact from the students, the efficiency with which you deal with those who step out of line—it all comes together perfectly smoothly."

I couldn't tell if my praise had affected the dean at all. He eyed me with a moderate expression from behind his desk. "I appreciate the recognition. Where are you going with this, Mr. DeLeon?"

"Well, as I pointed out, I've been mainly on the teaching side of things for quite a while now. I'd like to commit even more to making this school function as well as it can. I know I'm not on the same level as yourself and the established professors, but I was hoping that I could become more involved with your planning and general strategy. Any way that I can adjust my approach so that it provides additional support to your goals, I'd be happy to contribute."

They'd just have to tell me what those goals were in the first place.

Dean Wainhouse was silent for a long moment. I didn't think anyone would have noticed my association with Trix, which would have marked me as a potential problem to the staff. We'd been careful to keep our less professional interactions outside the school building, and now I was glad for that. The one time we'd really connected, we'd spent most of our time together wandering along the boundaries of campus and rambling through in the woods.

Finally, the dean rested his hands on the top of his desk. "I appreciate the offer," he said. "But I'm afraid I have trouble taking it at face value when I know you're a sharp and practical young man. You've been here quite some time. You may be looking for advantages to benefit yourself, which we can't count on continuing to benefit Roseborne."

Shit. I forced my mouth into a smile, more apologetic than enthusiastic. "I'm sorry if I've come across that way. I honestly think my contributions—"

"No thank you, Mr. DeLeon. I'm sure you can find your own ways to make a mark without riding on our coattails." He motioned toward the door.

The parting remark stung more than I'd been prepared for. My grandfather had said something like that too, when I'd been just a kid and excited about the idea of joining the company he'd built from the ground up in the decades since his family immigrated from Mexico.

I hadn't *really* wanted to help Roseborne's staff. The whole point of extending this offer had been to undermine them through my own means—to make a mark for Trix's sake and everyone else's too. The comment shouldn't have rankled at all.

But it did. Enough that I found myself marching back past the cafeteria to the kitchen the second I'd left the dean's office. There was another tactic I'd decided to experiment with since Trix had returned. Maybe I could still make a difference that way.

The students on kitchen duty were only just starting to bring in the dinner dishes for washing. I stepped in, ignoring their puzzled stares, and started scraping the remains of food left on the plates into a mixing bowl. It didn't take long before I had an unpleasant-smelling mess of peas, carrots, fusilli noodles, and alfredo sauce filling the bowl to the brim. I carried it out of the school and made straight for the outer wall.

The truth was, I didn't know much of anything about gardening. I couldn't remember my grandparents keeping even a potted plant in the penthouse apartment my sister and I had grown up in. But there were some basics that it was hard not to absorb somewhere along the way.

Plants grew better when fertilized. Decaying organic material became compost—that was fertilizer. In the absence of a compost bin, I was just skipping that step and spreading the scraps straight at the source.

The rosebush that clung to the campus wall was actually multiple plants that had grown tangled with each other. You couldn't tell where one ended and the next began other than by the spots at the base where a bit of stem dug into the earth. At each of those spots, I spooned some of my mixture of leftovers. A couple of days ago, I'd treated the left side of the gate. Tonight I tackled the right.

The gloop didn't look like anything that would help the flowers bloom better or longer, but it wasn't as if the staff were going to provide us with actual fertilizer or anything else that would encourage growth. They wanted to see us fade and fail alongside the blossoms. Maybe this gesture was completely pointless—I'd told Trix before that we couldn't change the health of the flowers by normal means—but I'd be damned if I didn't at least make an effort where I could.

I emptied out the bowl before I reached my own rose. No need to check on that one—no point in dwelling on its current state. If the flowers near my composting perked up more than those farther along, then I'd be able to tell my efforts had accomplished something.

Night was only just falling, the daylight dimming around me with the sinking of the sun behind the clouds. Normally I'd have wandered around campus for hours longer to pass the time until exhaustion dragged me up to the dorms. I set the bowl and spoon by the gate and meandered off past the carriage house, but a balking sensation swelled inside me. My steps turned heavier as the minutes slipped by.

What would I find Trix doing if I ran into her out here? Who would I find her doing it with?

I pressed the heels of my hands to my eyes as if I could shove away the images those questions provoked. They kept niggling at me all the same. Eventually, I went back inside, even though the other students were just heading up to the dorms themselves.

It only took a few minutes after I'd crawled into bed before I knew for sure turning in early had been a mistake. I closed my eyes, lying straight on my back under the covers, and the voices echoed through my head ten times as clear as the comments I imagined my grandfather tossing out during my waking hours.

His came first. *Don't be such a goddamned pussy, Elias!*

When you see something you want, you don't give a damn who else wants it too. You get right in there and make it yours.

My grandmother, with the audible Spanish accent she hadn't managed to erase the way my grandfather had his. *He only wants what's best for you. Can't you just listen to him? That's the least we can ask after everything we've done for you and your sister.*

Your mother would be ashamed to see you like this. It's a good thing she didn't have to live long enough for that.

A childish voice with a faint lisp. *Eli, you're going to look after me, aren't you? Isn't that what big brothers do?*

Like always, the questions and accusations came one after another in quick succession, no time to catch my breath in between. Partly memories, partly jabs that must have been inspired by whatever the school could sense was on my mind, all of it searing through my head.

I can do better, I found myself thinking, like I hadn't in years. *I'll prove to you I deserved all the chances I got. I'll prove to her that I'm the only one—*

A tremor ran through my limbs. Somewhere out along the wall, had my rose just shriveled a tiny bit more?

I gritted my teeth and pressed my face into my pillow. Before, I'd stopped wanting anything, and there'd been less for my curse to latch onto. Now I wanted too much. And that was exactly what Roseborne could use to wear down my defenses—and consume me for good.

CHAPTER TEN

Trix

$\mathcal{I}$ resisted the urge to squirm in the hard-backed chair I'd drawn up beside Professor Hubert's desk. The clock mounted on the wall was ticking loudly enough that I couldn't tune it out, and my face was getting stiff from the smiles I kept having to produce to convince her I was actually enthusiastic about the information she was giving me.

My commitment had paid off, though. When I'd shown up after seeing today's Composition class leaving the room, I'd managed to convince the professor to show me a list of the recent topics she'd had the students write about. Some of the ones at the bottom of the list stirred vague memories from times past. I could guess what *I'd* written about for those.

Hubert had gotten today's class to do some of their writing on papers separate from their notebook so she could evaluate them ahead of the presentations, and she was looking through those now with an impatient shuffling. I read over the list she'd offered up again, inspiration slowly coming together.

If I wanted to better understand her, and through her the rest of the staff, I should steer her toward a topic she'd have her own fairly deep feelings about. What did I know about the beings who ran this school? They lived to punish people and steal away their lives. Sometime in the past, I was pretty sure they'd engaged in enough violence to leave those bloodstains on the floor down below. That violence had probably helped them gain the powers they had now.

How could I work that into a Composition subject?

I mulled it over a minute longer and then said, "They're all awfully depressing, aren't they?"

The professor glanced up at me with an arch of her eyebrows. Again, that eerie sense of recognition ran through me, comparing the sharpness of her gaze to the girl in the photographs I'd spent hours studying.

"The most honest emotions come from our most difficult moments," she said simply. "You can't learn to express yourself fully until you're willing to delve into even those matters that are difficult to think about."

I nodded as if I agreed. "But still, I can't help wondering what you'd get if you had everyone write about a happier topic just once, now that they're used to all this."

Hubert's eyes turned thoughtful. Had she ever attempted that? To be honest, I was kind of curious how my classmates would respond. But I doubted she'd go for my suggestion as it was.

After a moment, she shook her head. "We still have much work to do. An easy assignment could interfere with the progress many students have already made. You'll have to trust my experience on this."

I sucked my lower lip under my teeth and nibbled at it, pretending to reconsider even though I already knew where I was going from here. "What if you combined the two—happiness and things that are difficult to admit? Like… writing about a time when we felt happy, but it was at someone else's expense?"

The professor didn't let her expression shift much, but she brightened a little at the idea. She rubbed her mouth, her gaze going even more distant than before. When she dropped her hand, I thought I saw it *tremble* for just an instant before she clenched it.

Had something about the suggestion bothered her even if she'd liked the thought of it too?

As I watched her, a niggling sensation crept up in the back of my mind, like one of those fragments of memory from my past times here drifting up from the deeps. I blinked, and an image flashed behind my eyes. Cool spring air, sunlight bright on the grass by the badminton courts. The girl with the dark hair and piercing eyes waving a long, curved object at her far side while she grinned sharply—at me. *Can you imagine, when they realize…*

I felt the sun's beams, tasted the fresh grassy scent in the air, heard her clear voice ringing in my ear as if I'd really been there, and then it was gone. I was nowhere but the hard chair in Professor Hubert's classroom, waiting for her to deliver a verdict on my proposed topic.

I swallowed hard, grasping the sides of the chair to steady myself. What had *that* been? It couldn't have been from my times here. The photos of those students had been from ages ago. As far as I could tell, the sun never shone on Roseborne now. The girl had been wearing one of those burgundy uniforms I'd never seen on campus other than in the photographs and the portraits based on them.

The tap of Hubert's finger against her desk brought me fully back to the present. "You know," she said, "there might be some value in that. I like the complexity of it." She studied me as if wary of taking any suggestion *I* made, which considering how much trouble I'd given the staff in times past wasn't surprising. "Are you sure *you'd* like to write on this subject?"

"The longer I'm here, the more I realize how much I still have to figure out about myself," I said in as genuine a tone as I could manage. "Maybe digging into past events will help me figure out what's happened to my brother now."

That answer appeared to satisfy her. She nodded and shuffled the papers in front of her. "Since the idea came from you, I expect to see particular effort from you with your own composition. This will not be the time to be slack in your commitment."

Her tone held an implicit threat. I'd already seen the pains she inflicted on students she felt had taken a cowardly approach to an assignment. I sat up a little straighter to show I'd caught her meaning. "Of course. Thank you for letting me look over all this. I feel like this is the one class here that really makes sense to me, even if it is going to be hard."

She couldn't stop the pleased smile that curved her lips at the compliment. She might still be wary of me, but not so much that having her ego stroked didn't affect her. "Go on then," she said, but not too brusquely. "I've got to finish up with these—and my marking system is going to stay private."

I was scheduled for lunchtime kitchen duty anyway. When I reached the cramped room with the old food scents that always hung in the air, Jenson and another guy were already there. The other guy was rinsing vegetables at the sink while Jenson chopped the ones already cleaned for a salad. I glanced at the meal list posted by the door and grimaced.

"Wieners and beans," the guy at the sink confirmed, seeing my expression. "The cans with the baked beans are in the pantry and the hotdogs are in the fridge, if you want to get started on that."

"Apparently the professors are sending us back to elementary school," Jenson said wryly with a deft swivel of his knife. "I feel fifteen years younger already."

The other guy chuckled and scrubbed at the carrot he was holding. "Maybe it'll be a little enjoyable in a nostalgic kind of way?"

"Knowing this place? Don't count on it." Jenson looked up with a sly glint in his eyes. "If you want to make things interesting, what do you say to adding some chili flakes to the salad dressing?"

"Hey," I protested even as my lips twitched with amusement. "I'd like to actually be able to eat that stuff. Whatever isn't already going rotten."

Jenson tsked and tipped his head to the other guy. "She's just a spoilsport."

I couldn't take much offense to the criticism when the fact that he'd been able to state it meant he didn't actually believe it. Rolling my eyes, I went to the pantry to grab the beans.

The viscous mess that poured from the cans gave off a pungent smell that made my nose wrinkle, and the hotdogs—a day past their best before—slid slimy out of the plastic packages, but after giving them a quick rinse and getting everything cooking in a couple of the kitchen's biggest pots, it at least appeared to be edible. Jenson kept up his casual banter with the other guy as we worked, occasionally shooting a grin or a wink my way.

He seemed to be able to hit it off with any of our classmates. I'd never seen him antagonize anyone the way he had me when I'd first arrived, and no matter who was around, he'd have them smiling and hanging off his words within a minute or two. Which was exactly the kind of thing that would have made me suspicious of him no matter what context I'd met him in. But with the things I knew about Roseborne now, I couldn't help wondering who he'd been before he'd ended up here. What crime did the staff feel he'd committed—and why had they chosen lies as his punishment?

I couldn't really ask him, even in a roundabout way, when he literally couldn't form an honest answer. So I just watched, absorbing this charming side of him with a tickle of attraction rising up alongside my curiosity.

When we'd finished, I wolfed down my own portion of the lunch quickly so I didn't have to worry much about how it tasted and then hurried back to the kitchen to get the clean-up over with. Taking over the washing meant I got to get out of here first.

There wasn't a whole lot of progress I could make on my main plan during the day, but in my search of the maintenance shed, I'd found an opportunity for a subtle show of defiance—and something that would let me pass the time here a little more pleasantly. Once I'd ducked into the small structure, I grabbed a trowel from the tool shelf and dug out the faded seed packets that had fallen into the corner beside that shelf.

I had no idea how old the marigold and columbine seeds were, and it was totally possible that none of them would sprout at all. I hadn't seen any flowers growing around the school other than the roses on the wall. But just knowing I was going to make the attempt energized me. Obviously at some point there'd been some sort of garden here.

I'd already picked out my spot: a stretch where the grass already grew thinner along the edge of the abandoned swimming pool, far enough from the school building that its shade wouldn't interrupt what meager sunlight penetrated the constant cloud cover. Sitting on the cracked tiles that surrounded the pool, I dug the trowel into the ground. Roseborne might have warped a lot of things, but it couldn't diminish the pure, heady scent of freshly turned earth.

Jenson must have come looking for me after he'd finished up in the kitchen. I was about halfway through clearing the stretch of dirt for the planting when he came ambling across the lawn. He stopped at the edge of my cleared area with a cock of his head.

"What are you up to now, Trix?"

"Seeing if I can get us a little more variety in flowers instead of just roses," I said with a brief motion to the seed packets lying beside me. "It's a longshot, but I figured, what the hell."

"Who can argue with that attitude?" He hunkered down across from me. "Any way I can pitch in, or is this a solo mission too?"

The reference to my dismissal by the laundry room prickled over me. I caught his eye. He didn't look concerned, but then, the more time I spent around him, the more sure I was that a lot more than just his words tended to lie.

There wasn't any reason I had to do this alone, though. "I'm going to need water after I plant the seeds. Do you know if the hose around the back of the school still works?"

"Let me find out for you right now."

He scrambled back up, loped across the lawn, and returned a minute later with the unspooling hose, its rusted nozzle gleaming with droplets. "Why not fill the pool while we're at it?" he said with a rueful smile that suggested he didn't really mean that suggestion.

"Sadly, I didn't bring a bathing suit."

"Oh, surely you can think of ways to get around that?" His gaze skimmed over me—briefly but with enough interest to spark heat under my skin.

I shot him a pointed look. "You can fill it up if you're willing to jump in first."

He laughed and sat back down to watch as I finished clearing the grass and turning the soil. "Is this something you do a lot?" he asked when I moved to the actual planting.

I guessed that hadn't come up in the past conversations that I couldn't fully remember. "Gardening kept me busy and out of the house," I said. Away from foster parents and siblings I'd preferred to avoid when I could. "I like that it reminds me that you can take the shit that's been thrown at you and use it to make something beautiful grow." I paused and looked up at him. "What did you get up to before you came here?"

Maybe I couldn't expect a clear answer, but I wouldn't get any at all if I didn't ask. I could tell from the twitch of Jenson's expression that he knew I meant specifically what he'd done to bring him here, not just in general. He tugged at a tuft of grass at the edge of my newly constructed garden. "Do you really want to get into that?"

"You know more about me than I can even remember telling you. Let's call it balancing the scales."

He let out an amused snort and lay back on the grass

to look at the clouds. "I had a charmed life," he said breezily. "I got whatever I wanted whenever I wanted it."

I eyed him as I covered another seed. "Did you?"

"Assume that's how I liked to think about it, anyway. Can a little smoozing and smooth-talking get you everything?"

"I guess not," I filled in for him. "But in your case it got you a lot."

He didn't argue, which presumably meant I'd understood him. "And of course I was always *completely* truthful when nudging people toward the things I wanted from them."

He'd lied, probably quite a bit, to manipulate the people around him? I could picture that, with a sinking sensation in my gut.

The curse he carried would be fitting for that, wouldn't it? He must have screwed someone, maybe a lot of someones, over with lies, and now he couldn't express anything directly even if he needed to.

"People got hurt?" I ventured quietly.

Jenson shrugged as well as he could with his back on the grass. "People can only blame themselves for not using their brains a little more to avoid falling for it in the first place," he said, and then winced. He'd obviously come to realize that justification wasn't actually true. "Don't worry about that, Trixie. Why should you when *you've* never fallen for it?"

His voice had gone raw in a way that made my earlier uneasiness fade. "No wonder I irritated you so much, then."

Jenson was silent for a stretch. He must have been figuring out the best way he was capable of responding. Finally, he propped himself up on his elbows so he could meet my eyes.

"Is it that hard to see that you're the only person I actually *like*?"

A lump filled my throat, so sudden and potent I couldn't come up with any words. It didn't matter anyway, because Jenson was pushing to his feet a moment later, brushing off his slacks with jerky movements as if he wasn't entirely comfortable with what he'd just admitted.

"I'd hate to miss being used for target practice in Archery," he said briskly, and gave me a jaunty salute. "Keep up the good work without me."

He sauntered off toward the school building, leaving me even more uncertain about how to feel about him than I'd been before this conversation.

CHAPTER ELEVEN

Jenson

For whatever reason, in all their wisdom, the wonderful staff of Roseborne had packed my afternoon jammed-full. I got out of the infirmary with my arm patched up where my Archery partner had clipped it just in time to start my shift on this week's bathroom-cleaning crew.

The last thing I was in the mood for was scrubbing down shower stalls and urinals. Checking the list of tasks under my name, I grabbed a rag and got started on the sinks, going with the least offensive option first. As I worked, I eyed the three guys who'd gotten the same assignment. From years of habit, my mind automatically skimmed through any useful detail I'd picked up about them.

Useful to me, that was. The pudgy guy named Jackman who was wiping the mirrors seemed like my best bet. It was only in the last few months that I'd had classes where I'd learned much of his story, but I knew enough to push the right buttons.

I let my sleeve fall back to reveal the bandage and "accidentally" stepped close enough to the other guy that his elbow bumped me when he lowered his arm. I jerked back with a pained flinch, even though the contact had only stung a little.

"Don't worry about it," I said nonchalantly as he turned to check on me. "Can't complain when the arrow could have gone right through my arm."

Jackman's eyes widened, probably with the experience of encountering an arrow that intimately before. He'd been here a while longer than me, so he'd had plenty of opportunity to enjoy all Archery had to offer. "Sorry," he said, despite—and most likely partially because of—my preemptive reassurance. "Are you sure you're okay?"

"Never been better! And delighted to get right back to work a half hour after I was bleeding all over the floor. Nothing better for building character, am I right?"

I said it with a joking lilt, and one of the other guys snickered, but I saw Jackman's shoulders stiffen like I'd thought they might. Whatever sin had drawn Roseborne's attention to him, it had something to do with being a total slacker. I'd gathered from his offerings in Composition class and Literary Analysis that his carelessness had meant he'd missed out on a lot—and disappointed a lot of people. From the way his voice shook whenever he talked about responsibilities he'd evaded, he'd been here long enough to believe he deserved this place.

And hopefully to want to be "better."

"They should have given you a break," he said. Not quite there yet, but guilt was one of the easiest emotions to hook.

"Ah, I don't mind," I said. "Putting in my time keeps me honest."

Jackman's expression tightened, and then he was blurting out on cue, "You've put in enough for today. I'll take over the rest of your duties in here."

I stared at him as if shocked. "I don't mind pushing through. I'd never ask—"

"You shouldn't have to. It's fine." He gave me a light shove toward the door, which was propped open to let out the fumes of the cleaning fluids. "You'll be doing me a favor. I've got more character-building to do."

He managed a small smile to go with the remark. I wavered for a second and then said, "Well, if you're sure...?"

"Absolutely. It's all covered. Go rest your arm."

Don't mind if I do. I gave him a grateful wave and stepped out of the bathroom to find Elias lurking in the hall just outside.

One look at his face told me he'd heard that entire conversation and had worked up some professional-level indignation about it. He crossed his arms where he was standing by the wall and gave me an authoritative glower.

"Problem, teach?" I asked. His slight wince at that blasé nickname always made it worthwhile.

"That's taking quite a risk, getting someone to do your work for you, isn't it?" he said.

I held up my hands, all innocence. "Hey, it wasn't my idea. I'd have happily kept going. How is it my fault if it makes someone else even happier to take the load off my back?"

His glower darkened. Lying came so naturally to me that I didn't think most of my classmates had figured out I couldn't do anything else, but somehow or other Elias had picked up on a pattern that gave it away. Maybe it was thanks to his apparent aptitude for math—whatever aptitude he had when the figures weren't constantly shifting. Maybe it was because of his leftover pride in his own dedicated if brutal honesty. It didn't really matter. It was just one more reason for him to think less of me. As if he wasn't just as fucked up in his own ways.

"We're all in an awful situation here," he said. "No need to make it worse for someone else."

"Think of it as me offering an opportunity. Do you think I'd go for it if the staff had ever showed they minded before?"

His lips pursed in distaste at the implication of how many other times I might have slipped out of chores. As far as I'd been able to tell, the people—if they were people—who ran the college mainly cared about class participation. As long as you turned up for your other duties at the expected time and the tasks all got done one way or another, they didn't give a shit how you accomplished that.

"I don't know what the hell she's ever seen in you," Elias muttered, turning away.

There was no doubt which "she" he meant. After the

admissions I'd managed to make to Trix just a couple of hours ago, the jab hit deeper than I should have let it. What the hell did I care what this prick thought of me?

And yet apparently some part of me did, at least when it came to the girl who'd grabbed both our attentions.

"What do you figure she's ever seen in *you?*" I shot back before I could catch my temper. "Some stuffed-shirt asshole who'd rather stick his self-important nose into other people's business than tackle his own?"

Elias's back went rigid, but he kept walking away, not even dignifying my insult with a backward glance. A trickle of nausea ran through my stomach. I should be better at keeping my cool than that. He wasn't worth the energy anyway.

Or maybe he was worth *more* than I was. Trix had seen something in him, after all. Had still wanted him around now that she had more of her memories. How would she have reacted if she'd seen the exchange we'd just had?

What would she have thought of my little trick to get out of bathroom-cleaning duty?

It didn't matter, I told myself as I stalked away. I was what I was. She could take me like that or leave me. I'd never pretended to be some kind of saint, and hell, the fact that I was here at all must have told her I wasn't one even before I'd given any hint about my past indiscretions.

She was probably still out there by the pool setting up her little garden. Trying to *grow* something in this godforsaken place. The staff would be pissed off if she managed it. I hoped she did if only just to see their reactions.

I was starting to think she really was going to take them all down in the end. And I—well, I guessed I'd be cheering from the sidelines. The professors had never been particularly won over by my charms, at least partly because they knew perfectly well when I was lying my ass off, and I didn't have a whole lot to offer in terms of revolutionary skills otherwise.

A class was just coming out of Composition, the eight students who'd been in there all looking kind of puzzled. I ambled over. One of them was a roommate of mine —Jerome.

"Hey, man," I said with a tip of my head toward the classroom. "What's Hubert got everyone pontificating about now?"

"She's getting more convoluted than usual," he said with a shake of his head. "And she wants us to talk about being *happy*—how do you figure that? Just sometime when what made us happy screwed over someone else."

I might have laughed if my stomach hadn't been clenched. So, the assignment was basically the entire last ten years of my life. I wouldn't have any shortage of material. Not that Composition class was ever that hard for me, since I couldn't confess much of anything in the first place. The trick was always working enough honesty into the false trappings of a story I came up with to convince the professor that I'd put in some effort.

"Sounds like fun," I said. "Can't wait to find out all about it when she lays it on my class tomorrow."

"I guess it should be a little interesting seeing what everyone else comes up with," Jerome said, and pulled a face. "I'm just glad I have a week and a half to figure out mine."

As he headed downstairs, the good humor I'd summoned for the conversation faded. I found my gaze sliding back toward the hall to the dorms where Jackman was scrubbing away on my behalf in the bathroom.

He'd made a commitment to changing his ways since he'd arrived here. I was still the same old guy, wasn't I? Was the difference that I'd always known I was a fraud and accepted it, and most of the other students had convinced themselves they weren't really hurting anyone until their flaws were shoved into the light?

If Trix did somehow break us all out of here... did I really *want* to stay the same guy I'd been? The guy who'd have flirted with her and cajoled her into bed if she'd been a little less skeptical, who'd have taken off on her as soon as I'd gotten my kicks and never realized what I was missing?

For fuck's sake. That jackass Elias had gotten too much into my head. I shifted on my feet with a restless urge and headed up to the dorms. Let's see if I couldn't write his crap back out of me.

When I sat down on my bed with the Composition notebook I'd retrieved from the chest underneath, my stomach clenched tighter. I gripped my pen so hard for a second that I was surprised it didn't snap.

Why not write the story of what could have happened with Trix if I'd met her a couple of years ago while I'd still been free? It would be a lie because it wouldn't really have been her—but also the truth because it'd been a whole lot of other girls I'd used and cast aside.

I brought the pen to the first blank page. The ink bled a little as I dragged the tip across the paper.

My senior year in high school, I met a girl who didn't trust anyone, and I couldn't resist the challenge. I wanted to get her into bed, and I knew to do that, I'd have to convince her I cared. But I didn't care about her.

I paused over the page with the deeper truth behind that statement ringing through me. The truth I'd half-assedly told Trix out by the pool.

I'd never really cared about anyone, not since the cops had locked Dad away and Mom had disappeared inside the gloom of her mind way back when—not until Trix had come blazing into my life. And if she ever understood just how true that was and how thoughtlessly I'd used so many people around me, she might blaze right back out again in an instant.

So I'd just have to be better, wouldn't I? And hope that'd be enough for both me and her.

CHAPTER TWELVE

Trix

There was a stretch of time between dinner and when the lights dimmed to encourage us to turn in for the night, and in that gap I couldn't do much except wait. Wait to head down to the laundry room when no one would see me to chip away at the wall between the basements. Wait until midnight crept close enough that I could grab some food for Cade and head out for another brief conversation with him.

Tonight, in the dwindling daylight, I found myself wandering along the stone wall, inspecting the roses I passed. Had any of them crumpled or browned more since I'd last checked on them? Would I find a new one now, one that was tied to my life somehow?

I couldn't see any obvious differences, but it'd only been about a week since Elias had first helped me discover the connection between the blooms and every student on campus. A matter of days since I'd found the one tied to my former roommate Delta fallen in dry scattered petals on the ground while her vacant body lay in her bed.

It looked as though someone had been attempting to tend to the bushes, though. A small pile of food scraps lay at the foot of each stem.

After I'd spotted several of those piles, continuing on along the sparse edge of the woods, I stopped and nudged one with my toe. The contents appeared to be the remains of some of our recent meals.

A twig snapped behind me. My head jerked up. Elias was moving between the trees to join me, a mix of hope and anxiety playing across his hard-edged features.

"I was trying to do some kind of composting," he said as he reached me. "I suppose I should have talked to you about it first. Laying the food down won't have hurt the roses, will it?"

"I don't think so," I said. "Honestly, I'm not sure anything natural we do will affect them one way or another at all, since they seem to be living—and dying—off supernatural power. But it can't hurt." I should have thought of trying something like that. It'd just seemed so absurd to create a regular compost heap when that would take weeks to produce any useable materials. Elias's more direct method might do the plants a little good, though.

I picked up a stick and sifted through the little heap, mixing a bit of dirt in with it. "The scraps will break down faster if you stir them up every few days. You want to be careful not to pile too much in one place at once, too. If we had some proper fertilizer... Hell, if we had proper *sun.*" I glared up at the clouded sky. "Most roses need a bunch of sunlight to really thrive. I guess that's proof of supernatural influence right there."

"I'll keep those tips in mind anyway," Elias said. "Not much point in doing a thing unless you're doing it as well as you can—even if it might not amount to anything in the end."

That wasn't the kind of attitude I was used to hearing from my classmates or coworkers or even my foster parents back home. Everyone around me had seemed to figure you were best off putting in as little effort as you could get away with toward your goals. But then, Elias had clearly grown up in very different circumstances from me, with much bigger goals.

"I'll bring around some water, too," I said. "That can help with the process. I've been watering the bush here and there anyway."

"I should have known you'd already have that aspect covered."

We studied the dark leaves and the thin spikes of the thorns for a minute in silence. "Do you think you're making any progress with Professor Hubert?" Elias asked.

"She's talking to me a little, and taking my comments into account," I said. "I don't know if that's going to get us anywhere useful in the end either, but—it's something."

"It is. I tried talking to the dean in my capacity as teacher but couldn't even get my foot in the door."

I tapped him teasingly with my elbow. "You're the one who told *me* to focus on the easier staff. Dean Wainhouse seems like a pretty tough cookie—he'd have to be if he's the one in charge of all the others. Why don't you go after Carmichael?"

His mouth slanted into a pained smile. "I also believe in focusing on your strengths rather than trying to work through your weaknesses. Warming people up to me clearly isn't one of my skills."

"It's not really mine either."

"Evidence would seem to suggest otherwise." He looked over at me, his dark brown eyes almost black in the fading light. "You broke through the walls I had up. Twice now. Helped me figure out that there were still ways I could live even though I'm stuck in here. I'd already realized what I'd done *wrong*, but I didn't really have a clue how to do anything actually right."

His words sent a giddy tingle through me even though I found them hard to believe. "I'm not sure I've been doing all that much right either." And what would this man with his studied control and practicality make of the horrible mistakes I'd made in a rush of reckless emotion?

"You don't give in. You ask questions other people are afraid to ask. I don't think you realize how rare that is here."

I gazed back at him, my heart thumping a little faster. Those observations were true, at least.

"You haven't given in either," I had to point out. "You still teach the math class as well as you can even though they've made it impossible." I paused with a sharper prick of curiosity. "Elias, when I confronted you about avoiding me during my last cycle here—you said things had gone wrong with someone I reminded you of. That you were worried the same thing would happen again with me. Was it me you were talking about in the first place?"

His jaw worked. "There wasn't any easy way to explain how I could know you and you didn't—"

"I understand that. That's not what I was getting at. Just... what about it did you think went wrong?" None of the bits and pieces of the more distant memories that he featured in came with any sense of anger or betrayal.

He hesitated for a long moment. Then he said, in a low voice, "I couldn't offer you much of anything in return. I couldn't get you out of here. I couldn't give you your brother back, not the way he used to be. I'm as trapped here as anyone else—a failure like everyone else here. Maybe even more so, because I thought I was some big shot before, and it turns out I was completely wrong. I didn't want to fail you all over again."

My throat constricted. I touched his arm, feeling the bit of warmth that seeped through the sleeve of his suit jacket. "Are you kidding me? You haven't failed at all. You answered my questions when you felt you could. You showed me the roses; you told me when I could speak to Cade. If I asked you to do something that would help us push back against the staff, even if it was risky, what would you say?"

"Yes, of course. But I should be able to—I'm supposed to be someone who can lead the way, not who sits around waiting for orders because I can't figure out what to do with myself."

"I think you've been leading the way just by surviving here as long as you have. What you've done with yourself is refuse to let Roseborne completely break you. That's why you're still here. And if you weren't still here, you wouldn't be able to help me any way at all."

Elias blinked at me as if that line of thinking had never occurred to him. Without warning, he leaned in, his fingers teasing into my hair, and kissed me.

My fragmented memories contained a few hazy kisses with him—and more. Those vague recollections had nothing on the vivid reality. Even as I sensed he was holding back at least a little, the press of his mouth commanded, the heat of his hand on my waist as he tugged me to him spoke of nothing but total assurance, no matter what his words had conveyed. I held on to him, kissing back instinctively, flooded with a hunger he'd woken up in me.

It was over sooner than I'd have liked. Elias drew back with a sharp exhalation. He gazed down at me, his lips parting as if he were going to say something, but then he closed his mouth again in a flat line. I'd have thought he was upset that he'd kissed me in the first place if the stroke of his thumb over my hair hadn't been so affectionate.

"I'm going to make sure I live up to every part of what you just said," he murmured finally, and motioned toward the wall. "Helping you take on Roseborne would be a hell of a lot more of an achievement than anything I accomplished out there."

I couldn't resist bobbing up on my toes to steal another kiss. Might as well take what I could get while he wanted this too, a selfish part of me said. But this time the feel of his mouth stirred an uneasy pang alongside my desire.

"Speaking of accomplishing things," I said when we eased apart again, "I should get on with my own plans."

No one was around on the first floor when I made it back to the school building. I lingered in the sitting room for a few minutes just to be sure none of the staff were wandering around and then slipped down the hall to the basement stairs.

My tools were where I'd left them last night after my first attack on the wall. I eased the dryer back with a slow but not too loud scraping sound and squeezed behind it. Sitting tucked away in there took me back to my earliest days with Cade, when we used to hide behind the Fricks' garden shed while our foster father raged. Huddled together with his arm around me and a reassuring murmur in my ear, or me watching him step out and take the worst of the man's rage when it'd looked like he might find both of us.

Now I had to step out to protect him. I hadn't had many opportunities to repay him in kind over the last twelve years. I picked up the tools with steady hands.

The hole I'd started carving in the wall there was already a few inches deep, as wide as my shoulders and equally tall. If the wall was only a foot thick, I'd be through it in just two or three more days. Dragging in a breath, I raised the hammer and chisel and got to work chipping more shards away.

By the time midnight approached, my legs were stiff from the awkward crouch I'd had to stay in and my shoulders ached from driving the chisel, but I'd dug the hole more than twice as deep. The work was going faster now with a little practice under my belt. I pushed the dryer back into place, stashed the tools, and slunk back upstairs to see what I could scrounge up for Cade in the kitchen.

I couldn't find much in the way of leftovers. After a few minutes searching, I wrapped up a hunk of cheese and some crackers that'd gone with the soup at dinner, which was the best I could do.

Outside, the wind had risen, rattling through the tree branches as I ventured into the woods. It whipped my hair against my cheek with a deeper chill than the constant mid-spring air usually held. I walked quickly, not bothering with my phone's light this time, more comfortable with the route now that I'd taken it the past three nights in a row. I'd wasted too much time in the kitchen, and I didn't want to lose any more of the precious minutes my foster brother got in human form.

I still wasn't quite on time. When I reached our usual spot, Cade was already standing there between the trees. His pale gray eyes fixed on me with even more intensity than usual.

"There you are," he said. "Got a little delayed?"

His tone was light, so maybe it was only my own guilt that sensed a criticism in that question. I held up the bag I'd tossed the crackers and cheese into. "I was trying to find you something decent to eat. Unfortunately, there wasn't much. I'm sor—"

Cade didn't even let me finish the apology. He stepped

forward and plucked the bag from my hand to toss it down by the roots of a nearby tree. "I don't care about what food you bring me. I just want to see *you*, Baby Bea."

His voice, husky but steady, slid over me like a caress. My skin twitched with recognition. I had to stiffen my legs against the impulse to back away from him.

"I'm here," I said. "Next time I won't let anything distract me from making it on time."

"I wouldn't want to become a chore to you."

"Of course it's not a chore," I protested. "I came to Roseborne for you. I've stayed for you, even when the staff might have let me leave. This is all for you."

"Is it? You've always had my back, haven't you, Trix?"

"Always," I agreed. Except for in those awful moments when I'd screwed him over in ways I hadn't even known at the time.

"And I've had yours." He touched my arm, running his hand up it to my shoulder. His fingers were warm and gentle, but they held me firmly. "I can get by alone. I have, pretty much, for months now. But it's better with you here. I wish I'd let you find me sooner."

I choked up abruptly. "Me too. I mean, I don't blame you, but—it was awful, not knowing."

"Poor Bea." His other hand lifted to cup my cheek, and I couldn't breathe at all then. He bent his head so close his lips brushed my cheek with his next words. "I want you with me every way you can be. Make the most of the little bit of time they give me."

My pulse hiccupped. I held myself in place, a twisting sensation rising through my chest. I loved him, and I wanted to prove it to him in every way possible. I loved him as a brother, and some of those ways never felt quite right, even if it gave me a thrill that *he* wanted me that much in spite of everything. But he deserved everything I could give him.

At least, sometimes he'd seemed to want me that much. The question spilled out. "I thought—the last time, you said it wasn't right, that we'd taken things too far, and you didn't want to ruin what was really important."

It hadn't been the first time he'd said that and then changed his mind, but he'd never sounded quite that emphatic before. He'd looked so determined it'd ripped my heart in two even with the simultaneous wave of relief.

"Going through all the shit this place forces on you has a way of putting things in perspective," Cade said, his voice soft and smooth as silk now. "Nothing's more important than you. Every part of you."

I thought of Ryo, and Jenson, and Elias just a few hours ago. Cade's thumb traced across my cheek to my lips. How could I say I was here for him if I wouldn't give him this? How could I deny that part of me was rejoicing that he'd turned to me for everything all over again? What did it matter if the rest of me balked?

Images flashed through my mind of the snatches of conversation and brief moments of closeness our relationship had been reduced to after Sylvie had come along. He'd swoop in, *It's been too long—I didn't mean to leave you lonely. Can't leave you with just those asses who are too dumb to realize that being a little screwed up doesn't define you.* A little chat shoulder-to-shoulder, half of a movie that happened to be playing on the TV, a sense of being lulled into security—and then his phone would *ding* with a text and he'd be off again.

How could I complain? He was still there; he still made time for me. No one else cared even half as much. But it'd still felt as though he was being torn from me bit by bit.

If I was his everything, then I'd never have to worry about losing him again.

He tipped his head, and I let my chin tip up to bring my lips to his.

CHAPTER THIRTEEN

Ryo

"All right, kids," Professor Ibbs hollered, her hands on her hips. She always called us "kids" even though the youngest student I'd encountered at Roseborne was eighteen. "Twenty laps around the school—and let's make it snappy."

She started her timer with a click, and I set off at a lope, falling into pace beside Trix. Gym was far from my favorite class, but having my favorite person on campus there made it more tolerable.

"How fast does she expect us to run?" Trix asked, her combat boots thumping against the lawn. I was lucky that I'd arrived at the college in sneakers that were reasonably suited to physical activity.

"Stick to the middle of the pack, and we're good," I said. "I don't think she has a specific time in mind—you just don't want to be at the back, or she'll decide you're not trying hard enough."

I could tell from the twist of Trix's lips that she could guess what the punishment for lack of effort might be. I'd been hit by Ibbs's retaliatory stomach cramps or dizzying headaches enough times to want to avoid them.

The one benefit to the perpetual clouds and damp air was we didn't have to worry much about overheating. The cool breeze flicked under my T-shirt as the fabric swayed with my strides. A couple of our classmates who'd initially taken the lead dropped back, the exertion taking its toll. You couldn't push too hard in the first few laps, or you'd burn yourself out before you were halfway done.

No one wanted to be left at the tail end of our jogging procession, though, so I couldn't slack off. My breath became ragged, making it difficult to say anything more to Trix. She looked as if she was focusing on keeping up just as intently. When we passed around the back of the school, her gaze slid toward the swimming pool and the patches of bare dirt she'd unearthed yesterday.

By the time we'd completed all twenty laps, my calves were burning and my shirt clung to my back with sweat. Ibbs yelled at us through a series of push-ups and sit-ups that would have been less uncomfortable on the mats in the actual gym room, ordered us to run through a row of tires she'd set up, and finally decided she'd harassed us enough for the day. "Take a walk and cool off," she said, and strode away without bothering to make sure we actually followed that last instruction.

I swiped at my forehead and wandered toward the

pool with Trix. She studied the plot of earth with a rueful smile.

"It's too early for anything to be coming up already anyway," she said. "But it'd feel like a real victory to see a little sprout in there."

"Soon enough," I said with easy confidence. If anyone could pull it off, it'd be her.

She glanced toward the woods then, and her expression darkened in a way I couldn't remember ever seeing before. Her body tensed slightly as if anticipating an insult or an outright blow.

"Are you all right?" I asked.

Her head jerked around. "Yes, fine," she said, faster than I could totally believe.

She'd seemed a bit distracted all morning, now that I thought back. I'd assumed she was just mulling over her various plans, but maybe knowing exactly how her brother had been consumed by the school was eating away at her. She might be beating herself up for not figuring out how to help him faster.

I couldn't contribute anything to those plans, but I could ease whatever stress she was carrying temporarily. "Come here," I said, giving her hand a little tug so she'd sit with me by the edge of the pool. "Nothing like a good massage after a workout."

"Is that so?" she said, her smile coming back, but despite her skeptical tone, she sat. I rested my hands on her shoulders and dug my thumbs into the trim muscles there until she let out a sigh that told me I'd found the right amount of pressure.

"Even if those old seed packets you found don't work anymore, we could probably find something viable in the groceries, right?" I said, letting my thoughts slip to easier problems than utterly overthrowing the powers that be. "Some of the fruits and vegetables will have seeds, and those will be—well, reasonably fresh."

Trix nodded, her head lolling forward automatically as I moved my hands toward the back of her neck. "That's a good idea. I'm not sure what we'll get that would grow quickly… Or germinate with so much cloud cover… but I could try a bunch of things. Even if just one starts growing, at least I'll have managed something."

"You've already managed a hell of a lot more than most of us," I had to say, and added, "I'll keep an eye out when I have kitchen duty and collect what I can."

"Thank you. That would be great."

I felt more than saw her mood change again in the shifting of her muscles under my pressing fingers, as if she'd drawn inward, away from me, for a moment.

"You don't have to do all this stuff for me, you know," she said. "I mean, I'm sure there are more interesting things you could spend your time on than searching the meal ingredients for seeds or whatever. Things that actually matter to *you*."

"Helping you out matters to me," I said. "Trust me, I'm not putting myself through any kind of torture here."

She made a dismissive sound and then just leaned into the massage for a few minutes in silence. As I worked my thumbs down her back on either side of her spine, she drew in a wavering breath.

"You've been trying to help me pretty much from the start, as far as I can remember," she said. "Even though I kept forgetting who you were, so you must have had to start over from scratch each time. Why not make friends with some girl here who'll still know who you are two weeks down the road?"

"You did end up fixing that problem," I pointed out, and she swatted my knee to say that wasn't enough of an answer. I paused, kneading my thumbs into her lower back and thinking of the first time I'd seen her, of our conversations during that initial cycle when none of us had any idea how she'd fit in here or what the staff would do with her. My chest tightened up.

"You were just so determined," I said. "And you're the only person I've encountered who's ever come here *knowing* there's something wrong with this place and willing to brave it for someone else's sake. That made you pretty different right from the start. I probably would have just admired you from afar, but I happened to stumble on you toward the end, when the things you'd seen were really getting to you and you were starting to think it was all hopeless—and somehow or other I managed to say a few things that reassured you. Until then, I hadn't really thought I *could* help anyone at all."

"I think I remember a little of that," Trix said quietly. I wondered which bits she'd retained. The memory was vividly clear in my own mind: Trix hunched over on one of the benches in the carriage house, the shaking of her breath bringing me from the doorway to her, the way she'd tensed at my hesitant squeeze of her shoulder and then leaned into me as if she'd been starving for a hug.

It'd felt like an honor to be allowed a rare glimpse of vulnerability beneath her defiant exterior, even if she hadn't meant to let anyone in. Even more of an honor when she'd smiled seeing me the next day and hesitantly warmed up to my attempts at friendly conversation.

And then she'd crossed some line the staff hadn't been willing to tolerate, and I'd lost the fragile connection we'd only just been forming. But the fact that she'd let me in at all had given me all the encouragement I needed to reach out to her again, to be what she seemed to need even if she hadn't yet shown it.

A swell of emotion rose inside me. I slid my arms gently around Trix's waist and tipped forward to kiss the bare skin at the crook of her shoulder where I'd swept aside her hair earlier. She set her arm over one of mine, her fingers gripping the back of my hand in a way that wasn't a rejection but didn't feel entirely encouraging either.

"I don't want to be a selfish person who just takes without giving anything back," she said.

A rough laugh spilled out of me. "You don't have to worry about that with me. There isn't a whole lot I can get out of, well, anything at the moment. You can assume I'm making the best of the situation that I can."

Trix swiveled in my loose embrace to look me in the face. "What do you mean about not getting much out of anything?"

I probably shouldn't have said even that much when I couldn't explain the penance Roseborne had enforced with any more specifics. "Don't worry about that either," I said. "It's mine to deal with—and I'm used to it."

She studied me with those light green eyes. "You've never said anything before about how the school is punishing you. That's what you're talking about now, isn't it? As much as you can reveal what they're doing."

I gave her a grimace that was the most direct answer I could offer, but the question in her gaze only got stronger. Maybe it'd be better if I laid it out as well as I could. Who knew what she'd imagine I was going through if I didn't? And then she'd know there wasn't any point in trying to make *me* happy in the first place.

"I told you that before I got pretty heavily into drugs," I said slowly. "And I did a lot of awful things, screwed things up with the people who mattered the most to me, because all I cared about most of that time was chasing the next high. Losing myself in the haze where everything felt so *good*. Well, back then, before I came here, I *could* feel really good. I could be just as happy when things were going well as I could be sad or angry when they weren't. I could get all kinds of pleasure out of life, even if I stupidly focused on just one."

I could almost see the wheels turning in Trix's mind. "But you can't now?" she said, her brow knitting. "You can't feel good—or happy, or whatever—about anything?"

I tested the words on my tongue to see what I could say if I was only confirming or expanding rather than stating it outright. Only vague terms came together into something coherent. "It's not completely gone. Just very... dulled. Compared to other, less enjoyable types of sensations, which there are many of here at Roseborne."

"So then..." Trix drew farther back from me, her expression shifting from puzzlement to something tighter. "All the stuff we've done together—when you kissed me just now—you haven't really been into any of that?"

Panic flashed through me. It hadn't occurred to me that she'd make a leap like that so quickly—or that she might feel betrayed by it. "No—I mean, I've wanted to, all of it."

"Because you liked the idea that you were 'helping' me. Because I'm some kind of project to prove you've gotten better."

"Trix."

She was already scrambling to her feet. I followed as swiftly as I could manage.

"It's not like that," I protested. Even if it had been a little, it certainly hadn't been all or even mostly that. "I like *you*. I care about you. More every time we get to be together. Any way I can make *you* feel good, I— It's—"

I couldn't force out any explanation that would sound right. The fact of it was that seeing her happy, seeing the pleasure I could set off in her, made me feel better than anything else ever had in this hellish place, even if the feeling was muted.

"I don't want to be some kind of charity case to you," she snapped when I couldn't finish my sentence. "I don't want you pretending to get off just to make me feel good about myself. You don't know me very well at all if you think I'd be okay with that."

She stormed off toward the school building before I could make another attempt at clarifying, although I might have only dug the hole deeper. As I stood there staring after her, I didn't feel much of anything but empty.

I love you, I thought. As much as I was capable of loving anyone in my current state.

But if I'd said that, after what I'd just admitted to, she'd never believe me.

CHAPTER FOURTEEN

Trix

The sitting room sofa wasn't any more comfortable than my dorm bed, but my bed was two stories up, and the sofa had been conveniently at hand when I'd finished dusting the foyer. I lay with my head propped on the stiff pillow, gazing up at the molded detailing around the edge of the ceiling and trying not to think about anything else.

"You look like you've had a bad day."

Violet's melodic voice carried to me tinged with irony. Wasn't everyone here having a bad day pretty much all the time? Compared to what the regular students went through, I wasn't sure I could complain.

I shoved myself upright enough to see her standing in the doorway, her dark curls falling loose around her face to partly shadow the scarred side, her arms folded over her chest. I couldn't tell whether she wanted some kind of answer to that statement or she'd just been trying to provoke me. My former roommate's temper was variable at the best of times.

"It hasn't been one of my best, that's for sure," I said. My thoughts slipped back to Ryo's face, so fucking *earnest*, as he'd told me that he didn't get any enjoyment out of being around me, that he *couldn't* even feel happy about anything we'd shared, and the hot prickling of embarrassment shot through me again.

I didn't know what was worse: that I'd somehow not realized he wasn't all that into me, just going through the motions, or that he'd thought just going through the motions was perfectly fine if it eased his conscience about the shit he'd done to other people before. Maybe both options were equally awful. Either way, the last thing I wanted was to see him again, but I'd only be able to keep that up until dinner time. A small school didn't allow many opportunities for getting some space.

He was better off without me anyway, wasn't he? I didn't have any idea what I really wanted either. Last night, with Cade... Had I betrayed Ryo and the other two by going along with my foster brother's advances? Had the tentative agreement that we'd take things as they came without worrying about commitments only included the three of them, or anyone I happened to end up kissing too?

My hand rose to the starburst scar on my forearm of its own accord. Cade had needed me, and I'd been there for him, like it was meant to be. What had I carved the matching birthmark into my skin for if I was going to hold back when he reached out to me? I owed him a thousand times more loyalty than anyone here.

Even if a gnawing sensation in the back of my mind insisted that kind of intimacy should be about more than loyalty.

We hadn't done that much anyway. Just a few kisses, his hands tracing down my sides, before he'd yanked himself back. I'd stretched out the conversation for so long before I'd given him what he wanted, it'd already been time for the monster to take over.

Violet hadn't moved, studying me as I emerged from that turmoil of memories and emotions. "Do you want to talk about it?" she asked, not sounding all that enthusiastic about the idea.

"Not... not really," I admitted, and considered her more thoughtfully. "Do *you* want to talk about something?" I wouldn't have expected her to approach me at all without some pressing reason, although I couldn't imagine what that would be right now.

"I guess I just wondered how you're doing." She looked awkward about the admission, as if there was something shameful in being curious about a classmate's wellbeing. I didn't think we'd really talked at all before my last cycle here, but apparently I'd made more of an impression than I'd realized. "You seem to be settling in pretty quickly. Any progress with the whole brother search?"

It must have looked a little odd to the other students that I wasn't as confused by the classes or constantly, anxiously badgering them for information the way I had the previous times I'd barged into their lives. I'd put on an act for the professors' benefit, but I hadn't bothered going through my own old motions when it was just me and my peers. Did they figure the staff had finally beaten the resistance out of me?

"I'm not sure," I said cautiously. "This place is pretty weird. Hard to get straight answers. Do you know anything about him?"

She shook her head like I'd expected. "Nope. Can't help you there. You've been keeping yourself busy anyway, though, from what I've seen."

That comment felt pointed, but I wasn't sure what she was looking for from me. Did she just mean things like my attempt at gardening and my interludes with the guys? Had she noticed my late night excursions even though we weren't sharing a dorm bedroom anymore? That was totally possible—the pain of her never-healing burns had driven her to the bathroom in the middle of the night at least once to seek relief in cool water.

"Better than being bored," I hedged. "You're welcome to pitch in with the gardening if you want." Especially since I wasn't going to turn to Ryo for kitchen seed collection now.

The corners of Violet's lips twitched with either amusement or derision. "No, I think I'm good on that front. If you get going with any other plans, feel free to let me know about those. Maybe I'd want to be looped in."

She walked off toward the front door, leaving me staring at her retreating back. That'd been an outright offer of help. I *definitely* wouldn't have expected that from her, even if she'd guessed some or all of what I was hiding.

But then, Violet had obviously been pretty miserable here. Why wouldn't she want to join forces if she thought I might have the key to getting out? No doubt she was offering in spite of her irritation with me rather than because she wanted to become besties.

I lay my head back down on the cushion, but the conversation had stirred up too many thoughts for my mind to drift away again. After a few minutes, I got up and headed for the staircase.

I was about halfway up the stately steps when my vision wavered. I stopped, gripping the bannister, as a hazy and yet piercingly insistent memory rushed through my head.

Two guys in burgundy uniforms came out the library door at the top of the stairs, jostling one another playfully. Something about that sight rankled... me? The image faded without any clue as to where it'd come from. It definitely wasn't from *my* memories any more than that weird vision I'd gotten when I was talking with Professor Hubert had been.

What had prompted it in the first place? I climbed the rest of the stairs cautiously, but no more impressions rose up. After a moment's hesitation, I pushed into the library.

It was empty, nothing but silence and the smell of old books. A shiver ran over my skin. I rubbed my arms, resisting the urge to spin around and hustle right back out of there. I hadn't spent much time in the library in recent memory, but when I'd come here for a Literary Analysis assignment, my reading had jostled loose all sorts of awfulness that I'd buried deep in the back of my mind. The wretched bits of my childhood could stay stifled, thank you very much.

But someone, sometime, had been annoyed by a couple of classmates coming out of this room? Was I picking up sensations from an actual person's mind or were they just delusions?

I crept deeper into the library, glancing around, waiting to see if anything in here might trigger a similar experience. Walking up and down the aisles only seemed to flood my lungs with more of that stale, slightly sour scent with the constant undertone of roses underneath. Like the books I'd searched through in Dean Wainhouse's office a couple of weeks ago, the volumes on these shelves looked several decades old.

Did they all date back to the time when students had worn those burgundy uniforms, when those sepia-tinged photos had been taken? What the hell could have happened here to freeze so much of the college in that period?

As I started down the last aisle, a prickling ran down my back. I slowed, scanning the shelves, the floor, the ceiling—

We can use it for whatever we want, a voice murmured across a distance I didn't understand. The images wavering before my eyes focused in on the bookcase at the back of the aisle. A hand reached to pop out the panel at the base of the bookcase. A bundle of cloth and a few papers lay in an indentation in the floor beneath it. *Just promise you won't tell anyone else...*

The voice and the image faded. My hands had gone clammy at my sides. I approached the bookcase and knelt down on the floor in front of it. Even if that trick had worked back—whenever that moment had come from— that didn't mean...

My fingers followed the same path I'd seen in the sort-of memory. I pressed a subtle notch at the right side of the panel. It flipped out so swiftly that my heart lurched.

There was the dip in the floor to create a deeper cavity, just like I'd seen. It didn't hold the same items as before, though. Now, I found a dried rose and a weathered softbound book too tall and thin for me to think it was a novel.

I slid out the book, finding the cover smooth beneath my fingers. An emblem was printed on the front: a crest with the letters RS and a rose mounted above them. Gilded lettering around it read, *Roseborne School Yearbook – 1927.*

I'd seen that crest before, hadn't I? On Cade's scholarship letter. Except it'd had a C instead of an S. This place hadn't always been a college?

With careful hands, I flipped the yearbook open. The black-and-white photos and the clothes and hairstyles fit the date on the cover. There was the building I was in right now but by full sunlight, which made it look more cheerful than I'd ever seen it. The badminton court in proper repair with a few players in the middle of a game. A car pulling up to the former carriage house. Rosebushes blooming on either side of the wrought-iron gate—but much smaller ones, only stretching five or six feet along the stones, the rest of which were bare.

And everyone looked so goddamned *happy*, or at least not miserable. Definitely not the school I knew now, even if it was technically the same institution.

It'd used to be a high school, I gathered when I reached the student photos divided by grade. A pretty posh one, from the jewelry the girls wore and the haughty smiles on so many faces. I skimmed over the freshmen and the sophomores without my gaze catching on anyone in particular. On the first page of juniors, I paused.

Someone had circled a couple of the boys and drawn a rough X across their faces. The pencil had dug in so deep it'd creased the paper.

The next page had another boy and a girl given the same treatment. I spotted a few familiar faces as well. Those two girls and that boy next to one of them, unmarked by whoever had gone at the others with their pencil, were from the photographs I'd found in the art room.

The seniors had fared worse than the juniors. Of the twenty or so of them, all of them had been crossed out except three I didn't recognize—and the other five students from the art-room photos. The girl who had a hint of Professor Hubert's necklace poking from beneath her collar stared up at me with her unshakeable gaze.

Everyone here deserves it, said a murmur in the back of my head. The same voice as in that strange memory that had led me to this spot. *But those ones—there's no point unless we get them.*

I held still, hoping more would come to me to explain what exactly I was looking at. When nothing emerged, I pulled out my phone to record every page in the yearbook from front to back. I couldn't risk taking it out of the library with me, but I intended to pore over it just as thoroughly as I had those portraits.

I might not know what the signs in front of me meant, but every particle in my body told me they contained so many of the answers I was looking for.

CHAPTER FIFTEEN

Elias

I was stacking the textbooks at the front of the room after class, the one act of my teaching "career" I could complete consistently and successfully, when Dean Wainhouse stepped into the room. He looked at me and the now-empty desks down his narrow nose, his blue-gray eyes even flintier than usual.

Had he ever visited me here other than when he'd first shown me to the room almost four years ago and announced that I'd now be teaching a class as part of my regimen at Roseborne? I couldn't remember it. I gave the books one last nudge and turned to face him. "Dean?"

"Mr. DeLeon." He offered me a thin smile. I was nearly as tall as he was, with enough muscle compared to his gaunt frame that I easily had fifty pounds on him, but somehow his presence was still intimidating. My stance tensed automatically.

He eased a little farther into the classroom, his gaze skimming over the figures on the chalkboard that I hadn't yet erased. "I thought, given your offer of assistance the other day, that you might be able to advise me on a small matter," he said.

Hope flickered in my chest despite my trepidation. Was he actually going to give me the chance to get into his and the professors' good graces after all? If this was some kind of test, I'd better make sure I passed it beyond any shadow of a doubt.

"Of course," I said in the smooth voice I'd have used for my business negotiations. "What can I help you with?"

The dean tapped his slender fingers against the aluminum chalk tray. "You see most of our students on a weekly basis. You also spend a certain amount of time with them in the dorms and cafeteria, where we interact with them far less. I was hoping to hear whether you've noticed any of them lagging behind in their... studies."

"Lagging behind?" I said, needing more than that. How could you lag behind in a class no one could ever succeed in to begin with?

Dean Wainhouse fixed me with a pointed stare. "Failing to live up to the potential we might expect from them here. Refusing to adjust their attitudes to suit their circumstances."

Remaining defiant, clinging to who they'd once been, no matter how noxious that person had been. My mind immediately leapt to my confrontation with Jenson yesterday, just down the hall—to the sly way he'd conned one of the other guys into taking over his chores. With the dean watching me expectantly, my mouth moved before I really thought it through.

"Jenson Wynter," I said. "He's still getting away with anything he can manage to."

Dean Wainhouse hummed to himself with a bob of his head, and just like that, I felt sick. I didn't even know what I was putting Jenson in for. Even if I didn't like him, he was one of the few people here Trix could turn to, however much he'd actually do for her. For *her* sake, at least, I shouldn't be throwing him under the bus.

Would I be even half as frustrated with him if he hadn't held some piece of her affection? How much had I adjusted *my* attitudes, really, if I started stomping on the supposed competition the second I saw something here I actually wanted?

"Mr. Wynter has been an interesting case," the dean said.

I groped for a remark that would soften whatever blow I'd dealt without backpedaling too obviously. I still wanted to seem like I was on the staff's side. "He hasn't been here as long as most of us, of course. I think it's only been about a year? It does take some longer than others to really absorb the lessons."

"To be sure. Nonetheless, I appreciate your insight. Are there any others you'd recommend we take a closer look at?"

An uneasy prickle ran over my skin. Did I want to toss anyone else to the metaphorical lions? Not particularly. I didn't talk with the other guys enough to really know how well they were coping, and it hardly seemed fair to name someone simply for staying quiet during my admittedly ridiculous math class. Hell, even Trix had acted much more compliant this time around, not that I'd have pointed a finger at her anyway.

"He's the only one who comes to mind off the top of my head," I said after a moment. "But if I notice anyone else who seems to be... struggling, I can let you know."

"That would be excellent. Keep up the work, Mr. DeLeon."

Not even "the *good* work," I noted as he walked out of the room. Why pretend that any of the work I did here taught anyone anything other than hopelessness?

I cleaned the chalkboard and headed out in time to see Professor Carmichael marching Jenson down the stairs to the first floor. The professor wasn't touching the guy, but it was clear from the set of Jenson's mouth and shoulders that he was capitulating under silent protest. My jaw tightened. I moved along the banister to follow their progress and saw Carmichael escort Jenson into the counseling room.

The professors didn't usually join us for those sessions. What exactly were they going to put him through in there?

Were they going to tell him that I'd been the one to suggest it? Did that possibility really bother me—or only the likelihood that he'd make sure Trix found out too?

You've got to cut away the dead weight, my grandfather said in the back of my mind. *Never feel any shame about clearing the way for what* you *need to accomplish.*

I closed my eyes for a second. What was I trying to

accomplish, then—winning Trix for myself or helping her break the spell on this place by whatever means necessary? Because what I'd just done had only contributed to the former... and maybe not even that.

That fact sat like a stone in my gut through the last couple of hours of the afternoon. When I ducked into the cafeteria to grab dinner, Jenson still hadn't emerged from the counseling room. I spotted Trix just sitting down with her plate and took my own out to the sitting room where I wouldn't have that additional weight loaded on my conscience.

Most days, I would have puttered around the school building as long as I could before heading out for my usual nighttime walk, but tonight I wanted to avoid any chance of having to face the people who could have accused me of wronging them in various ways. I meandered around the pool and through the carriage house, examining the tack on the walls as if I had any idea how those leather and metal pieces had fit together. My rambling trek took me through the scattered trees at the north end of campus, past the old gazebo, through the slightly hilly stretch to the west, and around into the thicker forest to the south. There, the scent of the roses thickened, filling my nose.

What did mine look like now? How much longer did I have before I went through that gradual weakening I'd seen come over so many of the students who'd been here when I'd arrived?

This once, enough clouds drifted away that the sky was almost clear. Starlight twinkled through the gaps between the leaves. I wandered among the trees until it almost felt as if I'd left the lump on my gut behind, until weariness turned my steps distant and made my eyelids droop. I turned toward the school building with a yawn nagging at my mouth.

As I came up to the edge of the woods, the moonlight caught on strands of bright orange hair tossed in the breeze. I stopped in the shelter of the trees.

Trix was striding across the lawn toward the forest with a determined air that made me frown. She didn't look so much like her usual defiant self, more as if she were girding herself for something she didn't really want to face. When she reached the woods, she hesitated for a second with a nervous swipe of her hand across her lips. Her shoulders squared, and she pushed herself onward.

I could guess where she was going. It was just after midnight, and I was the one who'd told her of her brother's brief human periods, after all. Before, she'd seemed relieved when she'd talked about knowing his fate and being able to reach out to him, though. Had he gotten worse since I'd last seen him? Had he *hurt* her in his beastly form?

I wavered for only a second before I picked my way back into the forest in the same direction Trix had gone. She felt responsible for getting Cade out of here—that much had been clear from the first moments she'd arrived on campus. If that devotion was getting her into some kind of trouble… Well, I didn't know what I'd do about it, but at least if I knew, I'd have the chance to do *something*.

The leaves rustled overhead. Now and then I heard the

crackle of Trix's passing in the distance. I knew the woods well enough after years of traversing them that it wasn't hard to make my way with barely a sound.

I'd just check that everything was all right—she could be stressed about all sorts of other things that had nothing to do with Cade, or simply because she hadn't made more progress yet—and then I'd leave her be.

Especially at this hour, Cade usually lurked in the deep center of the forest. The faint light from above dimmed more as the branches leaned closer together. At the sound of voices up ahead, I slowed, easing closer even more carefully until I could make out two forms in the twilight between the trees.

Two forms standing very close together. Trix was braced against the trunk of a broad oak, and Cade was leaning over her, his hand planted on the bark just above her shoulder. His head dipped so close that his nose almost brushed hers. A flare of jealousy shot through me before I could catch it.

They were foster siblings, not related by blood. There was nothing overtly *wrong* about that kind of intimacy between them. But Trix had never so much as hinted that she saw Cade as more than a brother. His poise right now was that of a lover.

I stepped back, ready to swivel on my heel and get out of there, when Cade's voice reached my ears, just loud enough to make out the words.

"You seem a little tense, Baby Bea," he said in a cajoling tone. "You know I'd never make you do anything you don't want to."

"Of course I know that," Trix said hastily. "I'm sorry. You don't need to stop."

"For fuck's sake. If you're going to talk about it like that—"

He shoved away from her, turning his back. Trix's mouth twisted with so much anguish it was obvious even in the sparse light. Despite my jealousy, my heart wrenched for her.

"I didn't mean it like that, Cade," she said, reaching to touch his back. "I want you. I'm here for you. You've got to believe that."

How could he not, when she'd given up her life outside these walls to come after him? But the guy didn't turn around. He shrugged dismissively. "It's fine. I'm not trying to push you. We can just *talk*."

Except he was pushing her. It showed all through the cold shoulder he was giving her now, the hint of a sneer he gave to that last word, the fraught look that crossed Trix's face.

I'd thought before that he might be hurting her, but I'd pictured that as a physical wound from a monster's teeth or claws. He was digging a different sort of dagger in. What the hell was he playing at?

How *dare* he treat her this way.

My hands clenched at my sides. "Please," Trix said, in a voice more plaintive than I'd ever heard from her before, a voice that didn't have any business falling from that girl's mouth. "Come back here. We don't have much time, and I—I want to make the most of it."

There was an awkwardness to the way she trailed her

fingers down his back that said she didn't really want *his* version of "making the most" of that time. If I could see it, then surely he could feel it. But Cade turned, nudging her back toward the tree again, and set a possessive hand on her waist.

"I'm still the guy who can see everything that's good in you," he said roughly. "Lord knows no one else ever paid enough attention. You've got me—and you're all I've got. All I want. I can't help it, Baby Bea."

"You don't have to. I'm right here."

Her shoulders stiffened as he dove in to claim her mouth, and my hands balled at my sides. I wasn't much of a fighter, but every muscle in my body was clamoring to burst in there and haul him off her. He was jerking her around, making her feel like she was doing something wrong if she didn't give in to his advances, like he was offering her more than anyone else would ever care to— and how long had he pulled crap like that if she didn't realize how wrong it was? He clearly knew just the right way to trample over her defenses.

The only thing that held me back was the knowledge that he knew her so much better than I did. If I interrupted them, I had no doubt he'd be able to spin that intrusion so I looked like the bad guy, maybe even that he was protecting her from me.

His head dropped lower to kiss her neck, his hand sliding up under her shirt, and I couldn't stand to watch anymore. My face flushed with a heat that was both uncomfortable and furious, I pulled myself away.

Who was to say there wasn't a reasonable case for

protecting Trix from me? Had I been thinking of what was best for her when I'd given Jenson's name this afternoon? No, only what was best for me.

Maybe I couldn't barge right into whatever dynamic Cade had her wrapped up in—but I could show her something better than that. I could prove that he'd been wrong when he'd said no one else paid enough attention to see her worth. I could show her how she deserved to be treated, respected.

At least, I'd damned well try my best, no matter how the voices in my head heckled me.

CHAPTER SIXTEEN

Trix

From the moment I'd left the library yesterday afternoon, the discovery of the secret yearbook had gripped my chest with a demand to be shared. But Elias and Jenson had been oddly AWOL for the rest of the day, and I wasn't inclined to turn to Ryo after our argument. I could have mentioned it to Cade, but we wouldn't exactly have had much time to discuss my findings—and he'd obviously needed something different from me anyway.

I hadn't squashed down my doubts well enough, and I'd made him feel like I wasn't really committed to him, to us. The memory made my stomach knot.

My restless urge to hash out my discovery with *someone* I could trust followed me as I showered and got dressed in the morning. My first instinct was to get Elias's input, since he had the most experience with the staff and a more analytical approach, but I hadn't run into him yet when I crossed paths with Jenson, who was coming up from basement laundry duty.

He stopped at the top of the stairs and gave me a smile that looked a little tense around the edges. We hadn't really talked since his comment about me being the only person around here he liked. He hadn't seemed all that happy about admitting it. Did he figure it would make me think less of him?

I didn't, and he was here. That made up my mind for me.

"Hey," I said. "Are you done with the laundry? There's something big I need to talk to you about."

His face brightened slightly, his stance slipping into a more casual pose. "Isn't it nice that I have a large opening in my schedule, then? Where should we chat?"

He knew as well as I did the risks of getting into anything we'd want to keep under wraps in this building. I was about to suggest the carriage house, since that'd worked well before, when another familiar figure emerged from the stairwell behind him.

"What's going on?" Ryo asked, hesitant but concerned as he glanced between me and Jenson and back again. "You sound like you found out something important."

His expression twitched when I met his eyes, but he held my gaze without faltering, as if to say he was here regardless of what had happened yesterday. I crossed my arms instinctively, but whatever else was true, whatever his motivations, I did know he wanted to help. And getting two outside opinions would be more useful than one. It didn't have to be anything more than a professional sort of conversation.

Why should I admit how much his confession had affected me anyway? I'd rather he thought I didn't care all that much.

"I'll explain in a minute," I said. "Let's take a walk."

As soon as I looked at the carriage house when we came around the school building, I knew it was out. That place held a few too many awkward memories, including a very clear one of a recent intimate encounter with Ryo. That was the last thing I wanted to be thinking about right now—the last thing I wanted *him* to be thinking about either.

Looking through the yearbook photos had reminded me of another structure on campus that I hadn't given much thought to before. Back in 1927, a wooden gazebo had stood at the edge of the lawn in the shade of a few elms. Over the decades, more trees and brush had sprouted up around it, and now it stood in the middle of a stretch of trees so sparse it felt a little absurd to call it a forest. But as we walked between them, they gradually blocked out the view of the lawns and the main buildings, giving us a little privacy.

Ivy had grown up the aged walls of the gazebo, the pointed leaves draped across most of the sides so thickly it might as well have been a wall. I climbed the three low steps into the shadowed interior and swept fallen debris off one of the built-in benches with my hand. Ryo let out a low whistle as he and Jenson followed me.

"No one's used this in a while."

Jenson looked as if he'd restrained himself from rolling his eyes. "What you mean is, it's gone the same way as the pool and the badminton courts and the carriage house? Where's the surprise there?"

Ryo let the snarky questions slide off his back. He sat next to me on the bench, leaving a foot of space where before he'd have scooted over right next to me. The careful distance sent a wobbly feeling through my chest.

"So," he said, "what's the news?"

As Jenson sank down at my other side, I pulled out my phone. "Since I started this cycle, I haven't just been remembering more about the times I've been here before," I said. "I think I'm also picking up someone *else's* memories, from way before that."

I explained about the hazy impressions I'd gotten with Professor Hubert and then around the library, and how the last of those had led me to the yearbook. The guys listened without any obvious skepticism. I guessed, considering all the craziness they'd already accepted at Roseborne College, a person absorbing a few vague memories that weren't really their own didn't sound all that ridiculous.

"I've been looking over the pictures, trying to figure out anything I can from them," I finished, bringing up the photos I'd taken on my phone's screen. "So far it's all still pretty confusing, which is why I was hoping you might notice something I haven't. You've both been here a lot longer than I have."

"Obviously something important went down in 1927," Ryo said.

"But what?" Jenson frowned at the images I was flipping through. "How the hell could *anything* turn this place into the hellhole it's become?"

"Supernatural powers are called supernatural *because* they don't make any natural sense."

"Thank you, Mr. Expert. That's so helpful."

"Hush," I said, giving Jenson a light kick to his ankle. "Look, this is the really creepy part."

I showed them the individual student photos in the senior section, with most of them crossed out. Ryo's eyebrows leapt up. "A bunch of the others, the ones that aren't X-ed out—those are the pictures Professor Filch gives us for the portrait painting contest."

Jenson nodded, peering down at them and then glancing at me. "Didn't you say you were thinking those seven—or eight, or whatever—might have been hurt somehow by the people who went on to run this school? What if they weren't victims at all? Wouldn't you cross out the people you *did* want to mess with, not the people you didn't?"

I shot him a relieved smile. "I've been thinking the same thing. Obviously we don't know exactly what happened then or how it created the situation we're in now, but I'm becoming more and more convinced that however the staff are connected to those kids, it was by mutual agreement, not something forced on them." I zoomed in on the photograph of the girl with the necklace. "I'm pretty sure Professor Hubert is wearing her necklace. And something about her... I don't know. Maybe I'm seeing things."

Jenson took the phone from me to examine it more closely. A pleased glint had come into his eyes at my agreement. "Don't sell yourself short," he said. "How can I not pick up the same vibe now that you've pointed it out? The others..." He studied one and then another and paused over one of the senior boys. His tone turned even more enthusiastic. "Don't you get a bit of that Professor Roth sourness from this guy?"

I leaned over to consider, my shoulder brushing Jenson's. He hesitated and then leaned into the touch. There was no denying the eagerness in his expression when he checked my reaction, his usual calculated front falling away to reveal something more genuine. Something I'd brought out in him.

It really meant something to him that I'd asked for his opinion, that I was taking it seriously. When all he could do was lie, how long had it taken before he'd started hungering to offer something real?

The boy he'd pointed out did have a bit of the jowly, houndish look of our Archery professor. Not so much that I'd have connected the two for sure, but then, I'd spent less than an hour in Professor Roth's presence so far.

"I can believe it," I said. "You'd be a better judge than me."

I smiled at him. Jenson blinked as if he hadn't expected anything like a compliment and then flashed a grin at me so bright it brought a flutter into my chest. A flutter and an ache somewhere between loss and longing.

Why couldn't this be so much more simple? Why did we have to have the weight of so much history, remembered and not, hanging over us—and on top of that, the tangled feelings Cade had left me with over the last two nights?

"Let me take a look?" Ryo asked.

I passed the phone over to him. "There are a few of the other photos that match the portraits in the juniors section," I told him. As he scanned the figures, my hand came to rest on Jenson's knee as if of its own accord. He didn't stir, but I felt his gaze shift to me again at the corner of my vision.

Underneath all the complications, I could at least show the simple fact that yes, I appreciated having him here. I didn't think what we'd already done was a mistake, even if I had no idea what it would mean in the long run.

Even if it was hard to imagine he'd still have wanted me all that much if he'd known I might be an even bigger mess than he'd ever been.

"I think I can see the Hubert and Roth thing." Ryo tilted his head to one side. "And this dude makes me think of Carmichael for some reason—not that he really *looks* like him, just…" He scratched the back of his neck. "This was almost a hundred years ago. Are we figuring these are their great-grandparents or something?"

"Who knows?" Jenson said. "What did you just say about the supernatural? If the professors can control where we go and what we talk about and how our bodies react, why shouldn't they have other weird abilities too? What if they're, I don't know, immortal vampires?"

Ryo made a skeptical face. "They do still get a little bit of sunlight without going up in smoke. As far as I know, they're not drinking blood from any of us. And wouldn't they look like the photos completely if they're the same people?"

"Jenson's point still stands," I said. "Maybe not vampires, but with the powers they have, they could have lived another hundred years, changed how they look, and who knows what else. Or the current staff could be descendants of these kids, like you said. I'm not sure how we'd figure that out." I motioned to the phone. "Do the names sound at all familiar?"

Each of the student photos had a name printed under it, but none of them matched Roseborne's current staff. The girl who seemed to be connected to Professor Hubert was Mildred Christoph.

Ryo considered each of them again, and then handed the phone over to Jenson when the other guy reached for it. Both of them shook their heads.

"Sorry, Trix," Ryo said. "I wish I could put together more of the pieces. Maybe I haven't been paying enough attention."

"The staff are pretty good at keeping their secrets," I said. "At least we know a little more than we did before. Maybe I can use this to prod Hubert the next time I talk to her, see if I can get anything useful out of her—or if it triggers more of those sort-of memories."

Jenson shifted his weight next to me. "Just stay on your guard, with her and the rest of them."

I raised my eyebrows at him. "Do you really think you need to worry about whether I can handle myself at this point?"

The corner of his mouth quirked upward, and his voice softened like I'd only heard once before, when he'd told me he'd never wanted to hurt me. "Do you really think I can stop myself from worrying about something happening to you, whether I need to or not?"

So much affection rang through those words that I couldn't tear my gaze from his bright blue eyes. It hit me then in a way it hadn't quite before just how much he'd been trying to protect in the last few weeks. Even when he'd been acting like an asshole, he'd been trying to protect me from the dangers of the school, yes. But how much had he also been protecting himself—from the pain of losing the closeness we'd shared that I'd forgotten, from the possibility of finding out I didn't want it again... and from having to face the intensity of feeling that showed in his expression right now?

He could have gone for it instead—turned on the wry charm I'd seen him employ so often with our other classmates, spun a few lies to draw me in with the inside knowledge from our past interactions. But he'd pushed me away, at least partly for my sake. Did he even believe he deserved the moments we'd had before?

A swell of emotion filled my chest. I touched his jaw to tug him into a kiss.

Jenson claimed my lips with a hungry sound that left no doubt about how much *he* wanted this, how much he'd been holding himself back. As the heat of his mouth flooded me, a sharper emotion prickled through the wave of desire.

He'd waited to be sure of me. He hadn't made any

moves on me without my encouragement, even after our make-out in the laundry room. Not because he wasn't completely enthusiastic, but because it mattered more to him that *I* was just as into this as he was.

Ryo was still sitting at my other side, but, well, let him watch. If it made him uncomfortable, he could leave. He couldn't begrudge me turning to another guy when he couldn't even enjoy anything we did together.

My hand returned to Jenson's knee with a teasing caress, and he let out a muted growl as he kissed me harder. His fingers grazed my cheek and cupped my shoulder—and another hand, tentative but steady, came to rest on my side with a stroke of the thumb.

A fresh jolt of heat shot through me from that point of contact. I eased away from Jenson to glance back at Ryo. He traced another gentle arc just below my ribs, his golden eyes gleaming.

"Nothing these days makes me feel even half as good as seeing *you* feel good," he murmured. "It still means something. And I'd bet two of us could make you feel even better than just one."

He made the offer like a proposition and an apology all in one. A lump rose in my throat. Had I jumped too quickly to assuming he saw me as a pity case, that this was all about pumping himself up with heroic generosity? The pleasure he got might be subdued, but I didn't think he could fake the desire that shone in his face right now.

Maybe I just wasn't used to the idea that anyone could want me the way I was, the way they were, without it all going wrong.

I drew in a breath and looked to Jenson. His mouth had twisted, but it slowly smoothed out into a smile that reached his eyes.

"Why not?" he said. "How can I say you shouldn't have everything we can give you?"

I gripped his shirt and pulled him to me. My other hand shifted back to rest on Ryo's thigh. Jenson captured my mouth again, and Ryo lowered his head to kiss the back of my neck. Their hands traveled over my body, Jenson's teasing over my ribs and up to the curve of my breast, Ryo's sliding around to splay across my belly. The flood of sensation from both sides nearly overwhelmed me.

I'd never felt *anything* like this before, not with any guy I'd been with. No sense of pressure to perform to a certain standard, to prove anything about my loyalty or excitement, just experiencing the moment with them, trusting that we all wanted the same outcome. So different from the casual hook-ups over the last few years.

So different from the anxious knot in my gut with Cade the last two nights.

That last thought sent a jab of guilt through me, as if I were betraying him by admitting the truth even to myself. Then Jenson stroked his fingers right over the peak of my breast and Ryo nipped the crook of my shoulder, and I gave myself over to the moment again.

Jenson drank in my gasp as he swiveled his thumb over my hardening nipple. With a click, Ryo undid my bra. All helpfulness, he tugged up my shirt to give the other guy better access.

As Jenson lowered his head to slick his tongue over my breast, Ryo nibbled a searing path from the corner of my jaw to my earlobe. My breath hitched. Pleasure radiated through me and collected in a burning need between my legs.

As if he could sense that, Ryo slid his hand lower. He ran his fingers over the fly of my jeans and then dipped beneath the thick fabric to caress me through my panties. A blissful quiver raced through me. I arched into his touch, into Jenson's demanding mouth.

Jenson sucked on my nipple so hard I couldn't hold back a moan. Then he trailed his kisses lower, down my sternum toward my belly. Ryo flicked open the button of my jeans, and Jenson yanked at them and my panties together. Then he was pressing his mouth to my clit with a confident swipe of his tongue.

An inarticulate noise escaped me. I sagged back into Ryo's embrace with the rush of pleasure, and he took the opportunity to turn his attention to my chest. He worked me over from the base of my breasts to the peaks with feathery touches while Jenson devoured my sex, and all I could do was cling on, one hand tangled in Jenson's hair, the other clutching Ryo's shoulder, adrift in the best possible way.

Somehow, I had it in me to want even more than this. When Jenson paused for breath, I wriggled the rest of the way out of my jeans. Then I pulled him back up over me. Ryo eased my head down into his lap, caressing my shoulders as Jenson and I kissed. I reached for him, but he only kissed my palm and brought my hand back to the other guy's shoulder.

All giving, no taking. But from what he'd said, maybe the giving was what got him off at all these days.

Jenson's cock pressed hard against the fly of his slacks. I stroked it through the fabric, and his breath stuttered against my lips. When I fumbled with the zipper, he kissed me even harder. The longing to be filled drowned out every other sensation inside me.

He paused for a moment after I'd freed him from his pants, gazing down at me as he slipped his fingers between my legs, not that there should be any doubt at this point that I was more than wet. His expression was so unlike the usual him, so *adoring*, that my heart skipped a beat.

"How can anyone be this beautiful?" he said, like he honestly couldn't believe it. He bowed over me again, tipping my mouth to meet his as he slid into me.

My knees came up instinctively to brace against his hips. He plunged a little deeper, and pleasure crackled through me like a wildfire. Ryo's hands kept stroking my shoulders, my sides, teasing through my hair, while Jenson thrust into me and I rocked with his rhythm, and the whole world narrowed down to the flames lit by these two guys.

This was what sex should be. Whether I deserved it or not, whether they'd still want me when they knew everything or not—no one should settle for less than this unrestrained bliss.

I bucked up, chasing my release, and Jenson blazed into me straight to the perfect spot inside. Just like that, I came apart, still swaying with him, shaking with the burst of ecstasy. He groaned and thrust harder, his mouth crashing into mine as he found his own release.

Jenson settled over me, his sweat-damp forehead tipped to mine. Ryo ran his fingers over my hair. Only scattered notes of birdsong carried through the rasp of our breaths. I clung on to the remains of the moment as tightly as I could, under the weight of the knowledge that whatever joy I'd found here might not last for long.

CHAPTER SEVENTEEN

Trix

As I approached the Composition classroom, my heart thumped faster. The test I'd planned was a tiny one that would only take a second, but it could have a hell of an impact on my time here—and how much more of that time I got to remember. If the professors realized how much I'd pieced together...

I had to keep it quick and quiet with plenty of plausible deniability. Act like nothing momentous had happened. Fuck, did I wish I had Jenson's practiced confidence to pull an act like this off.

I slowed near the doorway. Professor Hubert was sitting at her desk just a few feet inside, turned mostly away from me, her hand propping up her chin as she considered a piece of paper in her hand. I paused and then said, clearly but only loud enough that it should just reach her ears, "Mildred?"

Hubert's head snapped around in an instant, the heap of her hair swaying with the movement. Her pale face looked even grayer than usual. I ambled on through the doorway, propelling the follow-up I'd planned onto my tongue before she could react more than that.

"Hi, professor! Sorry if I startled you. I just had some other ideas I thought I could share with you."

She blinked at me, her shock turning her gaze more anxious than penetrating. "What did you say just a moment ago? What name did you call me?"

I stared back at her with the most puzzled expression I could produce. "A name? I didn't say anything until just now. There were some other students talking in the hall—maybe you heard them."

The tension ebbed from the professor's stance. She shook her head with apparent ruefulness, but her eyes stayed distant. "That must have been it."

I couldn't help nudging her a little more. "Are you all right?" From that reaction—you wouldn't startle like that hearing a relative's name. She'd responded as if she expected someone had been addressing *her*.

The woman—or whatever she really was—going by Professor Hubert now had once been Mildred Christoph. Had gone by that name recently enough that it still registered as hers.

So how was it she looked no more than thirty years older than a girl who'd been eighteen nearly a hundred years ago? Which of the other students had become which staff members? Was there an eighth presence on campus that lurked around us completely unnamed and unseen?

As I waited for Hubert's response, a crawling sensation ran over my skin.

"Oh, yes, of course," Hubert said with a dismissive wave. "What is it you wanted to bring up with me?"

The awkward moment had the side benefit of making her eager to change the subject. I was perfectly happy to let that work in my favor. I grabbed the nearest chair and pulled it over to her desk.

Had I set her off-balance enough that she might let something else useful spill? I gave her my brightest smile and said, "I was just wondering if you'd ever considered using topics to do with the school? I mean, rather than more general moments. It seems like it might be interesting to see what people make of, well, everything."

Hubert cocked her head. "Like what, for example?"

"Oh, I don't know, like... I mean, Tolerance class has to provoke some pretty strong emotions. That's kind of the point, as far as I can tell." I didn't have to employ any acting techniques to restrain a shudder. "Or even our surroundings—the building is awfully atmospheric, you've got to admit. And that rosebush that's basically taken over the wall..."

I watched her expression carefully as I listed off those possibilities. When I mentioned the rosebush, Hubert's mouth tightened. Her eyes hazed again, just for a second. "Better not to meddle too much with the roses, or they'll meddle with you," she muttered under her breath, and then laughed as if to cover that remark. "Well. Those are certainly some ideas I can take into account. You've gotten rather invested in this class, haven't you?"

She studied me even more carefully than before. For a second, I felt as if she were searching for something in my face. Trying to turn the conversation around to focus on me, maybe hoping I hadn't caught her momentary lapse. I shrugged, pretending I hadn't, but my thoughts spun. What exactly was her association with the twisted plant growing in the basement? That comment hadn't sounded all that appreciative of it.

But if she saw roses as something that could meddle with even her life, I obviously hadn't been wrong in thinking the bush downstairs was a key component to the staff's power. Maybe the real question was whether they were using it or it was using them.

"I think it's interesting hearing what people come up with," I said, and rubbed my arms as if this line of questioning made me uneasy. "It's gotten me thinking about a lot of things in my own life. Maybe... maybe we don't take a hard enough look at ourselves as often as we should."

Hubert gave me a strange glance that I couldn't read. It could be she was simply startled to hear me say something like that when I'd resisted the school's efforts to break me down so often before.

"I think that's absolutely correct," she said. "And it's a fact that I do my best to change. You can't grow from your mistakes if you refuse to confront them."

"You" not "we," I noted. Did she figure she'd never made any mistakes she should have to face up to, or that she'd faced up to them already?

Either way, she was done talking. She gestured for me

to put the chair back. "Class will be starting soon. Why don't you pick your seat?"

Not a problem. I'd already learned more than I'd dared to hope I would.

The sense of accomplishment and the lingering high from my morning interlude with Jenson and Ryo both faded the second I stepped into the woods by hazy moonlight. My lungs constricted a little more with each step toward Cade.

I shouldn't feel this way, not about him. He'd never forced me to do anything. *I'd* decided that showing how much I cared about him mattered more than how far I'd have wanted to take our relationship if he hadn't asked for more.

So why did the thought of telling him "No" now set off a flare of panic in my chest?

It wasn't as if I'd hated everything we'd done. A vague uneasiness didn't seem like that big a deal, not when he'd done so much for me—when he'd been the only person I could count on for so long. How much could I even rely on the three guys I'd connected with here at Roseborne anyway? Cade had always said we couldn't completely trust anyone but each other, and I hadn't met anyone who'd proved that wrong yet.

But I didn't want this. I didn't want to be kissed and touched and wherever else the brief time we had together tonight might lead if I went along with it from the start.

Not with conflicted uncertainty clutching my insides. Not with the memory of Jenson and Ryo devoting themselves to my enjoyment lingering so fresh in my mind.

The arguments chased themselves around and around in my head as I picked my way through the darkened forest. The breeze was absent tonight, the still air almost warm with its lacing of rose perfume and a hint of cedar from the trees around me. Other than the rasp of my feet and an occasional scampering in the brush, no sound reached me.

Then a mournful, moaning howl rose up so nearby that my legs locked automatically. A chill raced down my spine.

It wasn't half past midnight yet. Cade was still trapped in his monstrous form. At least, I assumed that had been him. Surely someone would have told me if there were other transformed students prowling around in the woods.

Whatever had provoked the howl, the melancholy mood appeared to have left Cade when I found him in our little grove. He walked halfway to me and then stopped, looking at me expectantly. Anything other than going right to him, he'd take as a rejection.

So I crossed the distance and let him wrap me in his arms. God, I *could* use a hug. I closed my eyes as I leaned into his muscular frame, imagining us back through twelve years of history when everything had been so much simpler.

"I didn't realize how much I missed having a real *life* until I had you in it again," Cade said in a low voice. "You make all the other shit here bearable, Trix. You and me were never meant to be pulled apart."

I opened my mouth to agree, but he was already nuzzling my cheek and claiming a kiss. His lips pressed against mine insistently, and this time even the quavering warmth his affection usually brought didn't spark. Every nerve in my body resisted, clamoring louder when his hand trailed down over my breasts to the hem of my shirt.

I eased my mouth back from his. "Cade," I said, quiet but firm. "I think—"

"What's there to think about?" His fingers teased up under my shirt to trace the curve of my breast through my bra. "You know how good I can make you feel."

My breath stuttered, but more with nerves than pleasure. He tugged me closer, an unmistakable bulge brushing my hip. My hands fisted against his shoulders. "It's just—"

His other hand dipped down to settle on the button of my jeans. "It's been torture, waiting for you. A whole fucking year. I need to be as close to you as I can get. I need to see you lit up like no one else ever could. *You've* gone without for so long. Let me remind you how it's supposed to be."

Those words echoed my thoughts from this morning so well and yet for all the wrong reasons—and all at once I was jerking back from him, holding him at arm's length with my hand braced against his chest, my pulse racing faster than a bullet train.

I did know how it was supposed to be. I had been lit up, more than I'd ever been with him.

Cade stared at me, the surprise and pain that flashed across his face so stark that my stomach flipped over. I'd hesitated before; I'd tensed up without even meaning to. This was the first time I'd put any real distance between us so forcefully. Guilt surged up through me into my throat.

"I'm sorry," I blurted out. "I don't think we should do that anymore. Not when there's so much else going on. We should be focused on how to get out of this place."

The excuse didn't soften Cade's expression of betrayal. "You know how much I've missed *you*, Baby Bea. I thought you'd missed me just as much."

"Of course I have," I said. "That's why I want to help you."

He took a step toward me, forcing me to drop my arm, his voice dipping low again. "This does help me. It helps both of us—remembering what we can be together. I shouldn't have thrown it away before—*I'm* sorry. It's never been the same with anyone else."

How much had I longed to hear those words when he'd first started dating Sylvie? My throat closed up. He was willing to give so much to me, so why couldn't I do this one thing that would make him happy?

"Maybe, after we're free from here," I heard myself saying.

He flinched. "You think you can do better than me. That's it, isn't it? You've let the guys who get to have you the other twenty-three hours of the day get into your head, convince you that they're worth something. Where the hell were they for the last twelve years? What have they done for you, really?"

"It's not like that," I protested, even though it sort of was. My pulse thumped on, dizzying me.

"You're always going to be the same girl you've always been, Trix," Cade said, his tone hardening. "Who other than me ever decided you were worth sticking around for? They're not going to be any different. You can't let them break us apart."

"That's not what I'm doing. I don't want to lose you, Cade. I just—"

I just needed to find the right words so he'd understand I wasn't really pushing him away. That I still loved him as much as I ever had. My mind whirled, stirring up a nausea that reminded me uncomfortably of the night I'd called Sylvie out, set up my little scenario meant to terrify her.

Everything had been slipping through my fingers, then and now. Cade had been slipping away from me. All I'd been able to focus on was groping for something, *anything* that might make a difference.

"You've just changed." Cade drew back. "It's been a while. You've had a chance to live your life without me. That's okay. It's good for me to see what I actually mean to you—or don't. We've always been honest with each other."

"Cade, please, listen to me," I said. "I want to love you like a brother. I *do* love you like a brother. That's all I mean. And I love you so much. You've been everything to me. I'd never forget that."

"I'm not just your brother," he said. "I proved I can be so much more than that. You could see that before."

I had. So many times, I'd let myself get wrapped up in

this not-quite-relationship we'd had to keep carefully secret. In a way, the secrecy had brought a thrill to it that made it more tolerable. Was it really fair that I was taking away now what I'd given before?

He was waiting, watching me with that hurt in his eyes. Part of me screamed to stop being an idiot and go to him, give him whatever he needed. Stop being so selfish.

I might have, if the breeze hadn't lifted then, teasing through my hair and over my skin like the other guys' fingers had just hours ago. My resolve steadied in the midst of the gale inside me. I clenched my hands and forced myself to say the words.

"I'm sorry. I don't want that right now."

Cade dragged in a breath as if to say something else, and his shoulders stiffened. We'd had enough of these late-night meetings for me to recognize the coming shift. His silvery gaze turned into a glower as a tremor ran through his body. "You threw away our time together for this. I hope it was worth it to make your point. But I forgive you. I'll always forgive you, Trix. I bet no one out there could say that and mean it."

His limbs shuddered. His back hunched. Before I had to see any more of the transformation, he hurtled away from me into the darkness where the forest grew thickest.

I stayed where I was for several minutes longer, hugging myself and gulping for air. Trying to convince myself that I hadn't just trashed the only thing in my life that had ever made it worth living.

CHAPTER EIGHTEEN

Trix

I'd been starting to think that Elias was avoiding me on purpose, reverting to the same tactics he'd used at the beginning of my last cycle here. But when I went over to the pool to check on my attempt at a garden after breakfast, just a couple of minutes later he came walking across the lawn to join me. The purposefulness of his stride left no doubt that I was his destination.

I watched him come through the bleariness in my head. Several late nights in a row had already been taking their toll, and after my argument with Cade last night, it'd taken me longer than usual to fall asleep once I'd made it back to the dorms. I had no idea how Elias managed with all his nighttime walks. Maybe he took lots of naps?

Despite my tiredness, I managed a smile. I'd been hoping to talk to him. The thought of how long it'd taken to make that happen sent a wriggle of nervous tension through my gut.

"Hey," I said when he reached me. "You've been a difficult man to find lately."

He winced, his head dipping with an apology that made me feel like a jerk for bringing it up.

"I'm sorry," he said. "There hasn't been much chance —I think it's better that we don't interact outside of class in the school. If the staff realize we've gotten friendly, they'll be a lot more suspicious of both our motives in digging for information."

Of course they would. I should have thought of that. But I hadn't—I hadn't even considered that the other professors noticing him being friendly with me might get him into trouble. I *was* a jerk.

"Good point," I said, the words spilling out more glibly than I'd meant them to. "We obviously need to come up with a secret signal to alert each other when we have something to discuss."

The joke didn't totally flop. One corner of Elias's mouth curved upward. He nodded to the stretch of bare earth. "How's this project coming along?"

That wasn't the most uplifting subject either. I held back a grimace. "No sign of anything sprouting yet. It *is* still early, but the seeds were awfully old. I'll probably need to resort to whatever I can retrieve from the kitchen scraps."

"The difference between those who succeed and those who fail is the former keep tackling the obstacles in their way and the latter give up," Elias said with a quoting air. I wondered who'd passed that advice on to him. I couldn't say it didn't make sense.

"I'll keep that in mind while I'm picking through the compost bin," I said, and brightened. "I have succeeded a little in another area, though." My gaze slid toward the school building, only thirty or so feet distant. I'd talked with the guys out here before, but my nerves had gotten jumpier. Being within sight of the building no longer felt all that safe.

Elias appeared to guess at my worries. He motioned for me to follow him. "Then naturally I need to hear all about that," he said.

We circled the pool and continued on to the west end of campus, where the grass grew taller and wilder until it hissed past my knees. When we'd left the school farther behind, Elias reached out and took my hand. His thumb skimmed over my knuckles in a gentle caress, and my mind tripped back to our recent kiss at the edge of the woods, to all the passion he'd let loose from beneath his disciplined demeanor in that moment.

What was wrong with me that I wanted to experience that all over again after everything I'd done with Jenson and Ryo in the gazebo just yesterday—and after shoving away Cade last night? How could I want all three of them and not give my foster brother the one thing he was asking me for? I still didn't even know how much of this sense of closeness I should trust. I barely remembered the more intimate times Elias and I had shared.

The ground rose slightly and dipped, and the school building disappeared behind that low rise. I turned to

Elias and bobbed up on my toes, bringing my hand to his jaw. Selfish or not, wrong or right, I needed some kind of confirmation of what I did remember feeling.

Elias's face brightened in the instant before he lowered his head to meet my kiss. His mouth melded to mine with all the giddying heat I'd been looking for. I had the same sense that he was holding himself back a little, that there were more layers of hunger and passion beneath I might have the chance to open up later, but what he did offer was more than enough.

He cupped my face as one kiss bled into another, tipping his head to bring our lips together at an even more blissful angle. The tenderness of his touch woke up a flutter and a pang in my chest. I liked that gentleness, and I wasn't sure I deserved it. It wasn't as if I knew how to offer much of the same in return.

The pang expanded into a sharp ache. I pulled back, my lips still tingling, and for whatever reason the first words that spilled out were, "I've been with Ryo and Jenson too. This time around. I don't know where any of this is going, and we did kind of talk about it that first day, but I thought you should know."

From the twitch of Elias's mouth, I suspected the admission had hurt him, even if he'd already known or suspected as much. "It's hard to ask for the regular rules to apply when it's not as if I can offer you any kind of future right now," he said. "You should—you should be able to take the time to sort out your feelings without us pushing you one way or another. And if it turns out one of them can give you more than I can, well, then that's how it is."

The strain in his voice suggested he didn't say those words easily. The ache rose to the base of my throat.

"It's not about who can give more," I said, gripping his arm. "You've all been here for me, with me, in *different* ways, and all of those ways feel important." I swiped my other hand over my face. "It's complicated, and I'm a disaster, so it's not really a surprise I'm not sure what I'm doing."

"You're not a disaster for being confused," Elias said, more vehemently than I'd have expected. He set his hands on my shoulders, gazing down at me. His teacherly air of authority combined with the desire in his eyes made something funny but delightful happen in my stomach. "Anyone who tells you that doesn't deserve the time of day from you."

What made him think I'd gotten that idea from anyone other than myself? Or that being confused was my only reason for thinking it? Imagining how he'd respond if I told him all the things I'd done with Cade, all the ways I'd hurt people or gotten people hurt, made my throat close up completely.

I hadn't wanted to talk to him to hash out my romantic feelings anyway. He didn't know what I'd learned about the staff from the yearbook or from Professor Hubert yesterday.

I dropped my gaze and reached for my phone. "I've found out some things. Maybe you'll be able to make more of them than the rest of us could, since you've been here the longest."

After I'd explained about the yearbook and my

conversation with Hubert, I handed him the phone to look through the student photos. Elias studied them with a thoughtful frown. "It's been a while since I saw these— the last time I participated in the portrait contest was almost two years ago. When you mention it, I see what you mean about those three... And this one." He pointed to one of the senior boys, a guy with a boxy face topped with messy black hair, deep-set eyes on either side of a prominent Roman nose. *Oscar Frederickson*, the name beneath said.

That guy hadn't sparked any sense of recognition in me. "Who does he make you think of?" I asked.

"Maybe I'm wrong. But there was this one time a while back when Dean Wainhouse was lecturing me about something to do with the math class... He got a little more worked up than usual, and I caught this glimpse of something in his face... I'm not explaining it very well, but as soon as I looked at that photo, it made me think of that moment."

"They've got to all be connected then. Somehow this Oscar and Mildred and the others became Roseborne's staff—and whatever else they are." I took the phone back from him and flipped to the juniors. "Do you have any idea about this guy?"

I hovered my thumb over an almost sickly looking boy whose pale hair stuck up in tufts across his head. *Winston Baker.* He was the only one from the photographs in the art room who didn't appear in the portraits. The school had just the seven regular staff members that I'd seen. What had happened to this one? He'd obviously once been a part of their group. But then, maybe he was still around in some capacity and I just hadn't stumbled on the full story.

Elias eyed him for a long moment and shook his head. "I think I may have gained at least a little good will with the dean. I might be able to ask him about that and get— maybe not a straight answer, but something that would help us put the pieces together."

My earlier guilt over not considering how our covert activities might affect Elias's standing surged back up. "Only give that a shot if you think you can get away with it without him becoming suspicious of you. I don't want *you* suddenly disappearing."

He gave me a smile that looked slightly pained. "I spent most of my life before I came here learning how to negotiate to get what I wanted. I won't tip him off."

The fact that my investigation was pushing him into old behaviors he clearly wasn't so keen on anymore intensified my guilt. "Then I guess you're the best man for the job," I said.

He chuckled and then glanced at the time on my phone. "Speaking of jobs, I'd better get back to the school or today's math class is going to be even more futile than usual."

I let him walk ahead of me as we came back into the college, falling farther back when I stopped to look over my supposed garden again. By the time I made it into the foyer, an impatient itch had tickled up inside me.

We were only going to get so many answers from the

staff. The full truth lay below us in the source of their power.

Laundry duty happened just a few times a week, and the students had just done the rounds yesterday. When I slipped downstairs, the machines were empty and silent, no one around. There wouldn't be more activity down here for at least another day. I could speed up my progress if I got a little more work in now.

I eased out the dryer as short a distance as I could get away with while still fitting behind it, retrieved my tools, and set to work chipping away at my hole. In some ways it looked pretty impressive now, so deep it encompassed my extended hand past my wrist, but I hadn't taken into account the fact that I'd need to expand the outer edge in order to carve the deeper parts wide enough all the way through. That had added at least one night's work to the task. If I could manage a couple of hours today, maybe I could balance out that loss.

The chips of concrete fell at my feet with a steady *tap-tap-tap* of the hammer and the crackle of a chunk giving way beneath the head of the chisel. In my tired state, the rhythmic pattern of it lulled me into a daze. I didn't hear anyone approaching until footsteps sounded right at the bottom of the stairs, just a few feet from the laundry room doorway.

"Did you hear that?" a girl said.

Shit. I wrenched myself out of the tight space behind the dryer, banging my knee on the side of the hole in the progress, and shoved the tools underneath the machine with a swipe of my boot. With as quick a heave as I could manage, I shoved the machine back toward the wall. It still jutted a few inches farther than the one next to it, but there was no time to push it all the way back into place or do anything else other than take a few steps away from it while brushing the dust from my clothes before the four girls from my previous dorm bedroom walked in.

They were all carrying small baskets of clothes. The girl at the front—Katrina, I thought—pursed her lips as soon as she saw me. "What are *you* doing down here?"

"I couldn't find one of my socks," I said quickly, thankful that I'd thought up excuses to have on hand. "I thought maybe it got lost down here. What are you all doing?"

She sniffed as if she didn't think it was any of my business. One of the girls flanking her made a face and said, "We missed getting our room's laundry out in time, so Professor Marsden told us to get it done now."

"So, why don't you get going?" the first girl added. "Whatever stupid things you're doing, I don't want you getting us in trouble because we happened to be in the same place."

I was trying to *help* them with the things I was doing, but I bit my tongue against pointing that out, or the fact that them being here at all meant they were obviously capable of getting themselves into trouble all on their own. "Next time make a reservation," I retorted, and brushed past them.

I couldn't go far, because I needed to fix that dryer. Leaving it even a little out of place was too big a risk. I puttered around in the storage room down the hall until I heard the girls' voices traveling away from me. When they faded away at the top of the stairs, I ventured out—and found Violet had hung back by the laundry room doorway.

"What *are* you doing?" she asked, her tone more baffled than it was accusing.

"I don't think you really want to know," I said, folding my arms over my chest. "Apparently most people here can't be bothered to try to make things any better."

Violet rolled her eyes. "I'm not great friends with the bunch of them either, but it's not that they're so happy here. It's easy for you to talk about changing things when you haven't seen how much worse the backlash can be."

I fixed her with my firmest stare. "Or maybe I do know, and I figure it's worth the possible consequences. But don't worry, I'm doing my best to make sure the blame doesn't fall on anyone who cares more about not rocking the boat." If I could, I'd make sure it didn't even fall on the guys who'd been willing to help me.

Violet looked back at me for a long moment. Her jaw worked. Then she turned and strode toward the stairs with a fierceness in her posture.

Great. A little while ago we'd been almost friendly, and now I might have made myself an outright enemy.

CHAPTER NINETEEN

Jenson

I almost missed Archery class because I wasn't supposed to have Archery in the first place. It was only by chance that I glanced at my schedule to confirm when my next kitchen duty was and saw the new addition, starting in less than half an hour. That was on top of my usual weekly arrow torture session scheduled just a few days from now.

Wonderful. Whose idea had that been? I hustled downstairs and found Professor Roth checking over the targets in the broad room.

"Mr. Wynter," he said when I came in. "I'm glad to see you're mended."

The scrape on my arm still stung a little when I took my shirt on or off, but otherwise I couldn't complain. That wasn't the point, though.

I waved my schedule at him. "Is it possible there's been

a mistake? Shouldn't I only have one Archery class this week?" Not being able to state outright how I felt about the extra class time forced a certain amount of politeness.

Roth didn't even ask to see my schedule to know what I was talking about. He meandered on to the next target without any sign of concern.

"You left your last class rather early on," he said. "We felt it was only reasonable that you attend another to make up for that time."

"We," huh? All seven of the assholes together? Had they made that decision at the same time they'd come up with the idea to lock me up in the counseling room for three hours straight?

The memory of that extended session was part of what kept my mouth shut. It hadn't just been long—they'd picked the most wrenching images they could. Girls I'd screwed around with sobbing to their friends, trying to figure out what *they'd* done wrong. Guys I'd conned out of money or work or whatever the hell else I'd set my sights on at the time facing eviction notices, getting kicked out by parents or partners, or patching themselves up after a fight I'd left in my wake.

And that didn't even get into the repeated reminder of the one guy who'd stepped right off a bridge after I'd weaseled my way into his life just long enough to steal his savings out from under him. Mom and Dad would have been real proud of that play. If I let myself, I could still hear the bloody smack of his body hitting the ground below.

I hadn't even known about any of the devastation I'd

left in my wake, not in concrete terms, until Roseborne had hit me with it. Never look backward—you didn't last long in the game if you let yourself worry about a mark after you were done with them. It wasn't as if they wouldn't have all screwed me over themselves if they'd realized they had the chance. That was what Mom had always said; that was what I'd always told myself.

Maybe it wasn't even true? Maybe the college had exaggerated the consequences to browbeat me with them? But that hadn't made it any more pleasant to see it all in vivid detail, made even worse by Professor Carmichael looming over me, questioning me about how and why I'd done what I had to every one of them.

I *could* be better than that. Even if I'd kept up some of the old patterns, I wasn't exactly the guy I'd been when I'd come here. And now I was a guy who'd given Trix at least a little insight that might help her—a guy who could show her a good time even if that included letting another guy pitch in…

I'd be so fucking good that no matter how much she found out about my past, she wouldn't care. It was that simple. Forget keeping a safe distance. I was not going to lose this girl—this girl who somehow seemed to want me even without a bunch of bullshit to smooth the way. I'd just have to handle what we had with as much attention and commitment as any con.

Professor Roth was watching me, waiting for my response. I gave him a winning smile. "That seems fair enough. Be sure that I'll endeavor to avoid any injuries today, although really that depends more on my partner."

"Choose wisely," he said in his gloomy voice, and turned away.

Since I was the first person there, at the moment all I could choose was which station I stood at. I took the one closest to the door so I could get my first pick of partner and practiced my stance with the bow, warming up my muscles, as I waited. I didn't want to be on the offending side of an injury any more than I wanted to endure another one myself.

My new classmates drifted in. I nodded to the first few and offered a friendly "Hey!" and a beckoning gesture when one of my roommates came in. Calvin had appeared to be decently coordinated. He came over to join me happily enough.

"If I promise not to spill any blood, will you do the same for me?" I asked with a smirk.

He laughed. "I'll do my best."

When we picked up our arrows and got down to the initial, tamer target practice, I couldn't stop my thoughts from drifting back to that recent Archery class with Trix—the first one I'd had with her since maybe her first or second time going through the paces here at Roseborne. The one where she'd refused to take a shot at me, even though with the way I'd been laying into her, it must have been a tempting opportunity.

I'd liked her since we'd ended up colliding a couple of run-throughs before that day, but *that* moment, when she'd dropped her bow and told off Roth in no uncertain terms—maybe I'd been falling for her for a while, but watching that had tipped me over the line to an utter goner.

As I retrieved my arrows and stepped back to let Calvin take a turn, an impulse prickled up from deep inside me. Why was I going along with this bullshit now? Why the hell did any of us? Everyone stood and watched, making their sneering remarks, while Trix demanded better—had we all given up?

Had I?

Just how much of a difference could we make if we all pushed back? It'd just take one person who could rouse a crowd to lead the way...

I'd fucked over a hell of a lot of people for my own gratification, as the professors had so kindly decided to remind me the other day. They wanted me to own up to my past mistakes? What better way to do it than to play sacrificial lamb for everyone else's benefit?

We cycled through another turn each before Professor Roth called for partners to take their spots at the targets. A mix of apprehension and anticipation washed through me as Calvin gamely offered himself up first. Professor Roth took his post near the door, crossing his arms over his chest. My pulse stuttered—and I smacked the base of my bow against the floor loud enough to get everyone's attention.

"How crazy are we that we're even thinking about doing this?" I asked, keeping my voice light but pitching it to carry. "Is there anyone here who *doesn't* think shooting arrows at each other is ridiculous?"

My classmates stared, but no one actually moved to

notch their first arrow. Roth scowled, his hands dropping to his sides. "Mr. Wynter, you—"

"I'm sure as hell not scared of what these jackasses might do to me," I said, wincing inwardly at the lie in that statement. I just wasn't scared enough to let it stop me. I tossed my bow toward the professor, who caught it automatically. "Do you really think you can make us take our shots if we all decide we don't want to? Go ahead and try."

I spread my arms. Someone behind me let out a startled giggle. Then my ears caught the most perfect sound—the tap of someone else setting down their bow.

I had only a split-second to enjoy it before Roth took me up on my suggestion. He didn't even move, but I had no doubt he was responsible for the lancing pain that tore through me from groin to sternum. My arms snapped around my belly instinctively, my legs wobbling.

"Is that the best you've got?" I managed to choke out. "How many students can the infirmary hold, anyway?"

Not that many, but definitely me. The searing agony dug deeper and gaped wider at the same time, as if all my organs were being hacked out with a dull knife. My legs gave, my knees smacking the floor. Professor Roth was demanding something in a raised voice, but the words blurred with the ringing of my ears. As I tipped right over onto the floor, I managed to angle myself so I could look down the rest of the room.

My classmates were all standing still, nervous but resisting, at least in that second. A small spark of satisfaction pierced through the pain, and then my mind went black.

I woke up at the sensation of the surface under me dipping. It took me a moment—and a lingering ache through my abdomen—for me to remember why I was lying on a mattress even thinner and harder than the one in my bed upstairs. The infirmary was dim, a patter of light rain hitting the small window, but I could make out the girl who'd perched on the edge of the cot with no trouble at all. It wasn't as if there was anyone else at Roseborne with that blazing orange hair.

"Hey," Trix said when I met her eyes. "How are you doing?"

"Not half as bad as the other guy," I joked, wishing that were true. After what we'd learned about the staff, I was starting to think I could have shot an arrow straight through Professor Roth's heart and he'd have simply plucked it out and accused me of misusing school equipment. I cocked my head against the pillow. "What are you doing here?"

"Everyone's talking about how you lost your mind in Archery. I know the standard punishment for that from experience."

And she'd come to check up on me. She'd cared enough to want to. Maybe my heroic stand had been intended as a selfless gesture, but I couldn't complain if it ended up benefiting me after all.

"You know me—tough as steel," I said, riding on that surge of elation. "It'd take more than one pissed-off professor to knock me down."

Even though I knew before I tried that it wasn't very smart, I couldn't help shifting to push myself up into a sitting position. My stomach screamed with fresh pain as I shoved myself upright. My fingers dug into the mattress, and some of my discomfort must have leaked into my expression despite my best efforts, because Trix grabbed my arm.

"Are you sure you should be doing that already?"

I managed a rough chuckle. "I already have, haven't I? Let's pretend I was the epitome of grace about it."

Trix's eyes searched mine. I didn't know if I was ever going to feel totally comfortable with the way she always seemed to pick up on more than I meant to say, but I could learn to live with it. I didn't want her to ever stop looking.

"You don't have to put on a show, you know," she said.

I arched an eyebrow. "What do you mean? Have you already gotten your fill of my undeniably charming self?"

She raised her own eyebrows right back at me. "No. But I like you best when you're talking to me like yourself and not like you need to lay on the charm no matter how you're actually feeling."

What I felt then knocked the air from my lungs and grabbed me by the heart. When had *anyone* ever wanted anything other than the charmingly jerkish front that'd become second nature to me? Did she even know what she was asking for?

It didn't matter. I tugged her to me, ignoring the fresh jab through my stomach, and kissed her like my life depended on it. Hell, it very literally might. But that wasn't why I'd made the move.

She had to know how much I cared too, even if I couldn't say it. Even if saying it would have been hard regardless of my stupid curse, thanks to all the walls I was used to having up. A nervous jitter ran through my chest, but I just kissed her harder, pouring all the adoration I had in me into the meeting of our lips. Then I hugged her, tucking my head next to hers and reveling in how much pleasure I could get from the simple act of holding her body against mine.

"So you're glad I came by, then?" she said, softly but with a bit of amusement.

I pressed another kiss to her temple and swallowed thickly. "Stay forever and we'll see how true that is."

Her shoulders tensed, but only for a second. Then she fully relaxed into my embrace. Maybe I'd said too much, revealed more than was really safe... but I was okay with that. Even if she ended up dropkicking my heart and stomping all over it in the end, I wouldn't be able to say the parts before hadn't been worth it.

CHAPTER TWENTY

Trix

When I came out of the infirmary, I was surprised to find Violet standing in the hall outside. She'd been leaning against the wall, but she straightened up when she saw me as if she'd been waiting for me.

"I heard what happened," she said. "Is he okay?"

Jenson really did have a talent if he'd convinced even the standoffish bomber girl to give a crap about his well-being. I nodded and allowed myself a hint of a smile at the thought of his heroics. Out of the three guys, he was the last one I'd have expected to make an overt protest against Roseborne's authorities. You couldn't really tell what people might have in them, could you?

"He's recovering and feeling very pleased with himself," I said, and remembered the brief argument I'd gotten into with Violet this morning. "I didn't put him up to that whole stunt, just so you know. In case you figured him getting in trouble was somehow my fault."

I mean, maybe it had been, just a little. If Jenson hadn't gotten real hope from seeing what I'd been able to accomplish by pushing back against the staff, he wouldn't have stuck his neck out. But it wasn't as if I'd asked him to take on the professors.

Violet's mouth slanted downward as it tightened. "I wasn't going to accuse you of that. Actually—" She glanced away, along the empty hallway, and then tugged her gaze back to me. "I shouldn't have criticized you this morning. I'm the last person who should be accusing other people of going overboard trying to stand up for themselves. Maybe I let that fact stop me from seeing the ways I could still make a stand now."

She'd told me my last time here about the crime that must have caught the college's attention: angry about being dismissed and teased by her high school classmates, she'd set off a bomb in the school cafeteria. She hadn't sounded all that remorseful about it at the time, but whatever Roseborne's staff had put her through once she'd gotten here must have at last convinced her that the act had been a mistake.

A big enough mistake that she'd squashed down whatever anger she had to feel here about the way she and the other students were treated. It couldn't hurt our cause if she recovered some of that anger now.

"I get it," I said. "This place is hard on everyone. I haven't had to experience half of what the rest of you have."

Something flashed in her eyes. "If I have much say, they won't get to inflict much on me anymore."

She spun and stalked away before I could ask what she meant by that, if I even wanted to find out. It was probably better if I didn't get her to spill her plans here in the school where the staff might be lurking unseen. Hell, maybe something like a bomb would be just what we needed. Were there materials around here we could use to blast open that basement door and spare me more chiseling?

I'd have to find a good, discreet moment to ask her. And a way of framing it that didn't give away how I knew she'd have any knowledge of bombs in the first place, in case she hadn't guessed the story behind my odd behavior.

I was feeling more hopeful myself than I had all day when I stepped out into the foyer and discovered that Violet hadn't been the only one waiting for me. Ryo got up from the sitting-room sofa he'd been perched on and gave me his usual warm smile, if a tad hesitant around the edges. We hadn't really addressed the admissions he'd made and the accusations I'd thrown at him by the pool the other day, even though our interlude in the gazebo must have given him some idea that I'd accepted his explanation.

"Who would have thought Jenson would turn crusader, right?" he said, his smile turning wry.

I had to laugh. "I was just thinking the same thing. He did a good job of it, though." From what I'd heard, Professor Roth had intimidated the rest of the class into continuing with their target practice—but only after several minutes of silent refusal through the painful punishment he'd inflicted on a lesser scale than he had with Jenson. It wouldn't have done much to reinforce his authority if everyone had gotten out of the task and simply had to rest up and recover.

Ryo paused and tipped his head toward the sitting room. "Come here?"

I went over to join him, and he took my hand to draw me down on the sofa next to him, sitting close enough this time that our thighs brushed together. He twined his fingers with mine and looked down at our interlocked hands before meeting my gaze.

"Are we okay?" he asked.

A sudden lump filled my throat. The intensity of his golden eyes told me how much my answer meant to him. The fact that I'd accused him of only caring about his own self-satisfaction seemed ridiculous now.

"Yeah," I said. "It was just—what you told me was hard to absorb in the moment. I've had people… change their mind about whether they really wanted me that way in the past, so I might be a little over-sensitive."

Ryo squeezed my hand. "I've never not wanted you. I don't know if it makes you feel any better, but when you've gotten used to not having very much of something, even a small amount seeping through the bad stuff feels like a lot."

Whatever muted enjoyment he got out of being with me, I had to assume he meant. And really, that made sense, even if I wished I could offer enough gratification to completely overshadow the miseries he experienced here, if only for a little while.

I didn't know how to say any of that, so I settled on, "I'm glad to hear that."

Ryo's smile came back. He leaned in, trailing his fingers along my jaw and down the side of my neck to send sparks shooting over my skin, and claimed a kiss.

I'd kissed all three of the guys I'd collided with at Roseborne today, and it was amazing how different it felt with each of them and yet how much I wanted to revel in all of those moments. Ryo could draw out the melding of our mouths until my heart was thumping for more. For a guy who couldn't take much pleasure in any kind of intimacy, he sure knew how to deliver it.

He'd never been a bad guy, not really, had he? He'd been bored and made some stupid decisions, and it sounded as if he'd done some pretty awful things while he was in the grips of his addiction—but it had been an addiction. He'd never *liked* hurting people or made the decision to do it with a sound mind.

Would he ever be able to understand how I'd plotted to terrorize a girl, gotten her killed, and let two innocent people take the fall for those actions without being under the influence of anything at all?

How could I have gotten angry at him for what he'd supposedly hidden from me when he'd at least owned up to it? My chest constricted around the idea of revealing all the things I'd done wrong.

I dipped my head to break the kiss. When Ryo gave me a

questioning look, I offered a weary smile that came naturally. "It's been a long day, and I didn't sleep well. I was actually thinking I should grab a nap before I, ah, get down to work."

Ryo's eyes lit up with a mischievous glint at my reference to my covert nighttime activities. "Go get some rest, then. We need you sharp."

I did actually go up to my dorm bedroom, but sleep didn't come easily. I lay there on the bed with my eyes closed but my thoughts whipping this way and that until my roommates started to enter to turn in for the night. There was definitely no way I was catching any Zs with them puttering around. Swallowing a grumble, I got up and went down to the bathroom to splash some cold water on my tired eyes.

At least I had something definite to focus on now. With the students heading up to bed, I could slip down to the basement to continue my work on the wall. In the laundry room, I set a quiet alarm on my phone and dug in, letting my mind narrow down to the warming metal in my hands and the crackle of the splitting concrete.

When the alarm went off at quarter to midnight, I froze. That was my cue to head out to see Cade. What would *he* have to say to me after last night? My body balked, my shoulders bracing against the solid back of the dryer.

I'd promised him I'd keep coming. Even if he was upset—*especially* if he was upset—I owed it to him to face him. Why shouldn't he feel betrayed when I'd turned him away at a time like this?

I just had to hope he'd start to understand that it

wasn't anywhere near a total rejection. That he could still count on me in every other way.

My gut balled heavy in my belly as I trudged up the stairs. I had enough time to put together a few scraps of food in a napkin, in case he'd want that this time. Then I set off with my chin held high and my jaw aching from the effort.

It'd rained for most of the afternoon. The clouds had eased apart, but the grass swiped streaks of moisture over my boots, and once I was in the forest, every stirring of the breeze sent chilly droplets down on my head.

Had Cade been able to find any shelter during the rain? I couldn't imagine him wanting to slink back to the school in his monstrous form, no matter what the weather was like.

Maybe he'd roamed over to the gazebo with its relative privacy, with no idea what I'd gotten up to there just a day before.

When I reached our usual meeting spot, there was no sign of my foster brother. I stood there between the trees, clutching the napkin that held the piecemeal dinner I'd brought, peering through the darkness. "Cade? Cade!"

I raised my voice as loud as I dared. No one appeared. It was already half past the hour. But if he had roamed farther than usual, maybe he hadn't made it back here promptly. How well could he even tell what time it was?

I stayed there, shifting my weight from one foot to the other, swiping away the flecks of moisture the murmuring leaves threw down at me. Five minutes slipped by, and then ten. My stomach was sinking when a familiar figure emerged from the shadows.

Cade held himself stiffly, his jaw set at a firm angle. He didn't say anything, just looked at me, his expression so cold I had to restrain a shiver.

"I brought you some food," I said weakly, holding it out.

He took the napkin from me without a word, without looking inside it. Something in his face shifted, like a crack in that icy mask, a brief twist of his mouth and drop of his eyes that showed the wounds underneath. Fuck. I hadn't meant to—this wasn't what I'd wanted.

My gut stayed knotted as I stepped closer to him, but I couldn't hang back. I touched his arm, gazing into his eyes. I'd comforted him before, but never over something I'd done. I'd never given him any reason to be this upset. He'd trusted me to be there for him.

"I'm sorry about last time," I said. "I meant it when I said it didn't have to change anything else. I'm still here. Will you please just talk to me?"

He gave a stilted shrug. "You didn't seem to like what I had to say before."

"It wasn't like that." I swallowed hard. "I love you so much. You've got to believe that."

I eased my arms around him in a hug. He didn't return the embrace, but he leaned into it just slightly. "Don't you know how much I love you, Trix?" he said in a low voice. "I've done everything I could for you from the moment you stumbled into my life."

"I know," I said, choking up all over again.

"Everyone else will always have their stupid ideas about who we can be and whether we're worth their time. You shouldn't have to put up with them judging you. Not when I'm right here. I want you no matter what you do."

Did he remember what I'd told him about Sylvie after all? His words clenched around my heart. Whatever bits of happiness I'd stolen with the three guys back at the school, they were only fragments. The three of them *would* judge me if they knew everything. Cade had always been right about that.

Why the hell had I let a little uncertainty make me push him away? Who was ever going to care about me and look out for me like he did?

Maybe I could fix everything as easily as raising my head and kissing him the way I'd denied him last night. But just the thought made my body tense up.

"That's why we stick together," I said, grappling with my hesitation. Had the time I'd spent apart from him and then with the other guys simply messed with my head? Why couldn't I just give him what he wanted?

How the hell could I say I didn't want it too when I'd gone along with it so many times before?

"That's right." Cade pressed a quick peck to the side of my head, and then, before I could make a decision one way or another, he eased back. He'd come so late that it must already be time for the change to come over him.

"We'll work this out," he told me as his back stiffened against the coming transformation. "You and me. Like we're meant to be."

"Of course," I said. Then he was stepping back into

the shadows with a ragged breath. I didn't think the shift was a pleasant sensation.

I turned and hurried the way I'd come, tears welling in my eyes and blurring my vision. What a clusterfuck I'd made of this entire situation. And I still couldn't get it together. I was off having my fun with other guys while he was trapped in a beast's body all alone... A shamed heat washed over me.

Even if I didn't want us to be lovers again, I'd come here for Cade. I couldn't lose sight of that, no matter how enticing I'd started to find anyone else around me.

As I snuck into the college's foyer, my gaze caught on a movement at the top of the stairs. Elias, presumably recently returned from his own late-night walks, was just heading into the second-floor hallway. The impulse shot through me to hustle up the stairs after him—

For what? To nab a few more kisses I didn't really deserve?

My legs locked. I stayed there in the darkened room for another minute, until the faint creaking of the floor faded. Only then did I dart up the stairs to make my way back to my own bedroom, alone.

CHAPTER TWENTY-ONE

Trix

A glinting gold circle flashed back and forth in front of my face. Four-year-old me stared at it, fascinated by the pattern of whorls and slanted lines that formed the sketchy image of a tree in its surface.

"Just watch this, little girl," my birth mother cooed. Half the time it'd seemed like she couldn't remember my name. "Watch it and get *very* sleepy."

"It's not going to work," my father muttered from somewhere beyond my vision. "It never works. Just leave her. We've got to get going. What's the worst that could happen anyway?"

"It was worth a try," my mom snapped. She gave the pocket watch a couple more swings before my eyes, but when I didn't fall into a hypnotic daze, she jerked it back with a disgruntled sound. "Fine. Stay here and just be bored then. It was up to you."

"I don't know why we haven't sold that fucking thing already."

My dad made a snatch at the watch, and my mom clutched it close to her chest. I'd never seen her so possessive of anything else, not even me.

"It was my grandpa's," she snapped, as if they hadn't sold every other scrap they could get their hands on that might have some worth, regardless of its history. They stomped out the door, and I sprawled on the floor to trace little pictures in the dust under the table and—

The dream wavered and lurched, and twelve-year-old Cade was standing over me, sunburned over his freckles, shaking his head as he let out a huff of breath.

"I *thought* you'd be able to keep up with me, Trix. Come on. Or are you so chicken you're going to make me go up there on my own?"

"It's just gross," I protested. "It's all full of spiderwebs and junk." And the last time I'd scrambled up into the attic crawl space, the ladder had fallen and I'd been stuck up there until our foster parents had gotten home, and Mr. Simmons had belted me across the back of the head so hard my skull had ached for days. Not that I wanted to admit I was scared of either of those possibilities to my brother.

"If they catch us, I'll say it was my fault. Come on. I know you're braver than this. Don't prove me wrong. What's the point if I don't have my partner in crime?"

Those last words released my legs. I found myself hustling after him as if I wanted nothing more than to poke around in the grimy shadows we hadn't yet explored.

I passed through a doorway—and my surroundings shifted. I yanked myself to a stop at the edge of a rain-slick courtyard, dark except for thin streaks of streetlamp light that seeped from the street beyond. A canvas leash dug into my palm as the Rottweiler I'd "borrowed" strained against it. Adrenaline thrummed through my veins, my heart beating so fast it was almost painful. Footsteps tapped toward us from the street.

"Here she comes," I whispered to the dog. "You go right at her—"

I snapped out of sleep with a hitch of my breath. The courtyard, the dog, and the dampness fell away. There was only pale dawn light touching the ceiling overhead, the rasp of sleeping breaths around me broken by a sudden whimper, and the ever-present perfume of roses tickling my nose.

My head still felt muggy. I rubbed my eyes and fumbled for my phone. It was barely six in the morning. No wonder my dormmates were still asleep.

I probably should have tried to drift off again myself, but when I closed my eyes, the image of Cade's determined face and cajoling voice came back to me. Something about it sent a thread of queasiness through my stomach. I sat up gingerly, careful not to wake anyone.

Since I was awake anyway, I might as well do something useful with myself. Chances were the whole school was still dozing.

I slipped down the stairs, considered the classrooms for a moment, and then breezed on past them. An urge to put myself face to face with my eventual goal had come over me. I padded down the hall past the professors' rooms on careful feet and jimmied the lock on the door at the end—the one labeled *Bushfell* as if that were the name of some staff member—with a hand so practiced now it made only the faintest click.

The door opened to the dim staircase that led to the padlocked basement door. A heavier silence settled over me before I set even one foot on the steps. I eased down one and then another, my mouth going dry. It took immense force of will to shut the door behind me so no one would realize it'd been opened.

Only a tiny sliver of hazy light crept from around the frame. I couldn't make out the door below me anymore. My feet scraped over the next step and another, my fingers clutching the railing. A faint vibration in the air tickled over my skin with the memory of the misshapen rosebush that lay just down the hall beyond—

And then a much more distant memory filled my head. Hustling down these steps by the light of a flickering candle, two boys and a girl ahead of me, unrecognizable from behind. *Hurry up*, one of them said. *We have to make sure everything's ready, or there's no point.*

They'll be damned sorry, another mumbled, his shoulders hunching.

My feet thudded on the concrete steps, and a clammy sweat was trickling down my back. A question seemed to have stuck in the back of my throat. *Do you really think…*

I—whoever I was in that flash of the past—opened my mouth to say the whole thing, and a hand closed on my shoulder, jolting me back to the present so abruptly that a yelp slipped from my lips.

I flinched and jerked around, my spine smacking the wall in the narrow space. Dean Wainhouse glowered down at me, looking even taller and spindlier than usual standing on a step above me. The door at the top of the stairs, the one I'd carefully closed no more than a minute or two ago, stood wide open again.

"How did you find yourself down here, Miss Corbyn?" he said in a somber voice.

How had he *known* I was down here? Had I made more noise than I'd realized?

Had something changed, and my presence in the school wasn't escaping the staff's notice the way it had the first few days?

I scrambled for an excuse. I'd gotten so used to being able to sneak around the school undetected that I hadn't taken the time to come up with one first.

"I was having trouble sleeping, so I was just walking around a bit, and I looked down here and saw the door was a little open," I said, as convincingly as I could, with a wave toward the doorway behind him. "I thought it was one of the professor's rooms—that it must have come open by mistake and they'd appreciate it if someone closed it for them. But when I came over, I saw the stairs—I was just wondering what's down here. Are students not allowed?"

"I'd have thought the padlock would have been a clear indication," the dean said. It was hard to tell from his grim expression whether he'd bought any of the rest of my admittedly flimsy story.

I rubbed the back of my neck as if in embarrassment. "Yeah, I guess it should have. I'm sorry. I've just been trying everything I can to find out anything about my brother—it's hard to shake that habit."

Dean Wainhouse eyed me for a moment longer, but he seemed to decide my offense hadn't been egregious enough to bother with a punishment. That would be revealing more of his hand than he might have wanted to —so far I hadn't given any of the staff reason to inflict their vicious magic on me.

"Now you know this area is off limits," he said stiffly. "Out with you, and find something better to do with your time."

He marched back up the stairs, and I hurried after him. Even after being caught, stepping out into the light sent a rush of relief through me. Whatever exactly had gone on down there, whatever still did, I didn't need a guide book to tell me it'd been nothing good.

"I'm so sorry," I added with a bob of my head, and headed down the hall at the dismissive wave of the dean's hand. The skin down my back quivered, as if struck by the same clamminess that had come over the past student—I had to assume—whose memories I'd been tumbling into.

Were they all from the same past figure? I could be picking up fragments from different former students each time. If I could get more control over it, look at "myself" in those moments clearly enough to get some sense of my —their—identity…

If I could make more of them rise up at all. They hadn't been very predictable. I couldn't think of any pattern of triggers that I could try to provoke again.

Especially if the staff would catch on to me lurking in any parts of the school I wasn't meant to be in.

Part of me wanted and yet dreaded the idea of testing whether that was true. If the dean or one of the professors found me poking around somewhere else I wasn't supposed to be right after I'd been investigating their secret basement, they'd start watching me like a flock of hawks.

Instead, I went upstairs, showered to wake myself up a little more, and came back down to the sounds of the breakfast duty crew clanking dishes in the kitchen. Jenson emerged from the infirmary while I hesitated outside the still-empty cafeteria. His cinnamon-brown hair was even more rumpled than usual, and the smile he shot me was a little sheepish.

A twinge of affection filled my chest. There'd been something so frank in the way he'd turned to me last night when I'd come to visit him—I wasn't sure how many people had ever gotten to see that stripped-down side of him. Hints of it showed in his expression now.

"I would have *loved* to go back to the dorms," he said as he ambled over to join me, sarcasm playing through his voice, "but I found myself glued to the bed. Can anyone argue with one night's sleep in actual privacy?"

As uncomfortable as I'd found the infirmary cot was, I could see his point. "Might as well take advantage of it while you can," I suggested, smiling back at him.

"Who'd have thought you'd see things exactly the way I do? I knew there was *some* reason I liked you."

I made a face at him, and he smirked back at me, but there was no edge to it at all. The same sense of devotion I'd felt from him last night tingled over me. An unexpectedly pointed jab of uneasiness came with it.

He was joking around because he didn't think I was actually anything like him—like the guy he'd been out in the real world who'd strung people along with his lies. I'd let him keep thinking that. I'd asked him to drop the front that he obviously felt most comfortable with and be real with me.

How real was I being with *him*? How many lies of omission had I already told by skirting around the truths I'd rather not share? And that was on top of the lies and evasions I'd kept up back then with Cade and our friends and, really, everyone.

A chill pooled in my gut. I managed to keep smiling, but my throat closed at the same time. Jenson cocked his head, maybe picking up on the shift in my mood, and all I could think was that I had to get out of there before I made myself even more of a liar.

"I—I meant to check on the garden before breakfast," I blurted out. "I'll catch up with you again later."

Then I bolted for the front doors before he could offer to come with me, my conscience snapping at my heels.

CHAPTER TWENTY-TWO

Ryo

I didn't know what was up with Trix, but she was definitely more skittish than usual. Since it was her first Literary Analysis class in this iteration of her time at Roseborne, she didn't have to present any commentary, but her expression stayed tense through the entire hour. When Professor Carmichael handed out our reading assignments for next class, she didn't even glance at hers before folding it and stuffing it into her purse.

I'd gotten to class just shy of late and hadn't been able to grab a seat next to her. As we headed out, I slowed my steps so that she would catch up with me just outside the door.

"I feel like this class should actually be called Psychoanalysis, the way he's obviously prodding at our issues," I said under my breath with a smile to show I meant it more as a joke than a rant. "Which works out well, since about half of the other classes here seem designed to make us more unstable."

Trix's lips twitched, but then she pursed them as if her automatic response bothered her. "No kidding," she said. "Have you ever—"

She cut herself off, her gaze sliding away from me.

"Have I ever…?" I prompted.

She shook her head. "Never mind. I was just thinking I actually prefer Composition to this class, even though Composition is theoretically more to the point."

I thought I might know what she meant. My hand reached for hers instinctively, but she stepped away before my fingers found hers. I couldn't tell if she'd even registered the gesture.

"Lunch duty," she said with a grimace. "I'll see you."

She headed down the stairs, leaving me feeling weirdly bereft. If I couldn't even make her smile, add a little levity to our mutual imprisonment here, what use was I?

Okay, now I was being a sad sack. What did I expect her to do—skip her assigned duties to hang out with me? Anyway, I had this new assignment I might as well take care of while she was otherwise occupied.

Knowing that the powers that ran this school had used the space to hide some of their secrets made the library feel even more eerie than usual. The thump of the heavy door behind me shut out all sound from the hall, and I always thought I caught a hint of rot under the normally comforting smell of the old books. And that wasn't even getting into the emotions the room tended to stir up, which I suspected was what Trix had been thinking of when she'd mentioned preferring Composition.

My last assignment had been pretty on the nose—a scene where a belligerently drunken man had berated his wife to the point of tears. Not hard to figure out what associations Professor Carmichael had hoped I'd make there. Maybe this one would be a little tamer. As long as it didn't have anything to do with addiction or substance abuse, I'd be happy.

I found the book and leaned against the shelf opposite while I flipped through to the assigned chapter. The first line made me take back that last thought.

The tires screeched as the car veered into the opposing lane.

My stomach lurched; I jerked the book toward me, pressing it against my chest as if hiding the words would will them away. Would stop them from echoing through my head with the all-too-vivid sensation of a massive structure of steel spinning out of my control, the honks and the laughter turning into shrieks, the thunderous crunch when the vehicle rammed into its final obstacle...

The taste of blood trickled through my mouth as though I'd bitten my tongue. Only a memory, but so freaking real. I wet my lips and swiped my hand over my face, finding the sheen of sweat that had broken out on my forehead.

Fuck Carmichael for stirring that horrible moment up again. Fuck him for assigning me to say anything at all about it.

And fuck me for bringing it about in the first place.

That was the point of all this, wasn't it? To keep rubbing our shit in our faces until we admitted how much we stunk.

I gritted my teeth, squared my shoulders, and forced myself to look at the book again. Line by line, page by page, I took in the scene. Not like mine so much. A country road rather than a freeway. Smacking into a tree rather than colliding with another car. The passenger injured but whisked to the hospital in time, not... not...

Even with the differences, the images from my memory flooded up alongside the pictures drawn by the text. By the time I reached the end of the chapter, my breath was coming rough. My fingers clenched over the last page.

I wasn't going to need to read this again. The narrative was burned into my mind with all the force of the parallel one the professor had intended to provoke. So it wouldn't hurt if I did *this*.

I wrenched out one page and then another, wincing at the grating sound of each tear. The memories kept stewing in my head, but my hands knew how to work without much conscious direction. They ripped and folded, twisted and ripped again.

When the haze behind my eyes cleared enough for me to pay attention, I'd formed two paper dolls, complete with protruding hair and noses and separate clothes folded tight around their bodies. Their tiny hands interlocked in a way I had to say looked defiant.

Looking at them steadied me again. I was making up

for the past. I was *making* things, period, instead of leaving only wreckage behind me.

I tucked the figures into the torn section of the book, like a counterpoint to the message the words printed on them had given me. Then I shoved the book back onto the shelf and walked out, my legs only a little wobbly under me.

The satisfaction I'd gotten from that minor act of creation and rebellion only carried me for a short while. Trix didn't come out of the kitchen during lunch hour other than to bring out the platters. I guessed she ate in there while getting a head start on the clean-up. After I finished, I wandered around the school until I had to admit to myself that I wasn't accomplishing anything other than hoping I'd cross paths with her so I'd have something happier to focus on.

Enough of that, Shibata, I told myself sternly… and ended up wandering around outside instead. The air was still damper than usual after yesterday's rain, the ground lightly soggy beneath my feet, the grass squeaking with the pressure of my sneakers. Trix's garden remained bare earth, but I didn't have a clue how to convince anything in it to grow anyway. Looking at the rosebush along the wall with its scattered blooms only made my stomach clench up.

When I meandered toward the carriage house, I discovered that a few students had gathered on the patchy badminton court. The nets sagged between the rusted posts, most of the fabric disintegrated, but it looked like the two guys and two girls had found some old rackets and a couple of birdies somewhere. And when I said "old,"

I didn't mean fine antiques. Several of the intertwined strings were snapped, and the wooden frames looked battered, at least a couple of them cracked in places.

The two duos were determined to get at least a little entertainment out of the things, though. I leaned against the side of the carriage house to watch as they faced off on either side of the desolate net. I'd never played badminton except when forced to in high school gym class a few times, and from the way this bunch held the rackets, I was going to guess that was about the extent of their experience too.

They had dedication—I'd give them that. They gamely batted the first birdie back and forth, stopping with minimal grumbling when it got stuck in a gap in one racket or when another racket started to bend a bit too much and its holder paused to fiddle with the frame. But there was really only so much they could do.

After several back-and-forths, the birdie snapped apart with a puff of dust, and no amount of tweaking and glowering could force it to reassemble. Just a couple of exchanges into their attempt with the second birdie, the frame on one of the cracked rackets split completely, leaving it wobbling beyond the point of usefulness.

The girl holding it swore and flung it on the ground, and the group fell into a murmured discussion that I guessed was about whether there was any point in continuing their game. As if Roseborne would have allowed us even that minor enjoyment. Hell, I wouldn't be surprised if the place had conjured up the equipment for someone to find specifically so it could frustrate them.

That was what we were here for: to be ineffective and reminded of our wrongs until the powers that be had sucked all the hope out of us.

In that moment, my current attitude descended on me like a cloud, and a sour taste filled my mouth. Was this who I really wanted to be? Some fatalistic loser who stood around just waiting for the dreadful inevitable, not wanting to *let* myself hope for anything more? How many people had I spread that gloom to, just by drifting along and assuming that nothing could be changed, over the last few years?

I'd been willing to accept that Trix might make some kind of a difference. Why wouldn't I believe—*expect*—the same thing from myself? Even if I never left the college, it'd be a hell of a lot better to waste away here knowing I'd brought some brightness to as many of the lives around me as possible. Helping Trix didn't absolve me of all my sins.

The other students were just trudging out of the court, their posture defeated. My gaze fell on the broken racket, and an itch spread through my fingers.

"Hold on," I called to them. "I might be able to fix it up. Let me check out the other ones too."

They gave me skeptical looks, but the girl went back to retrieve the broken racket, and they all tramped after me into the carriage house, which I'd found was the more promising source of materials on campus. I sifted through the grooming equipment and pieces of tack until I found a roll of steel wire at the back of a shelf. That would do.

My sometime-classmates watched with increasing

avidness as I clipped off sections of wire and twisted them around the cracked areas on the racket frames. I added a similar length to the other side of the oval to balance out the weight, and curved the ends into little curlicues because I could. Might as well add a little flare while I was working. Then, with the clippers and waxed thread I'd discovered in the back room before, I trimmed the frayed areas of the strings and rewove them.

With each motion of my hands, a sense of purposefulness came over me. Maybe this wasn't exactly the work I'd imagined doing before meth had taken over my mind, but it had the same essence. I was restoring objects so other people could still find worth in them. As jobs went, that wasn't a half bad one.

If Trix could thumb her nose at the school with her garden and her other schemes, if Jenson could tell off Professor Roth to his face, I'd be an ass if I didn't let myself stage my own minor revolution.

"That's awesome," one of the guys said when I handed him a repaired racket. He turned it, examining my efforts, and shot me the kind of grin I didn't see around campus very often. "Nice work, man. Thanks."

The others murmured their own expressions of gratitude and headed back to the court with more spring in their steps. I watched them go with a smile of my own. I didn't think this glow would fade anywhere near as quickly as the one from my hasty paper dolls would.

What else was there around here that I could fix? I took in the stalls with a more considering eye, ready to take on my next project.

CHAPTER TWENTY-THREE

Trix

My thoughts kept swinging back and forth as I made my familiar midnight trek through the woods. I had to settle things with Cade once and for all, make sure the full truth of my fuckups was out in the open, and take whatever the fallout was. He deserved to know—that was why I'd told him in the first place. The rest didn't matter compared to the fact that I was responsible for him ending up here.

I should have to own up to *someone*. Maybe I didn't owe a confession to the other guys after the short time they'd been in my life, but I definitely owed it to Cade.

A pinch of fear drove another line of thinking along. I'd tried to tell him once already. He might already know. If he didn't, wouldn't I just be causing him even more pain after I'd rejected him and made him feel he didn't mean as much to me as I did to him?

It would be so much easier to let that sleeping dog lie. To focus on rebuilding our connection however I could.

I still hadn't completely convinced myself one way or the other when I reached our usual meeting spot, right on time. At the sight of the empty, moonlit grove, my heart stuttered with the thought that Cade might be hanging back again. But a moment later he stepped out of the darkness, with a crooked smile so like his usual self that I choked up just seeing it.

"We really got ourselves into a mess, didn't we, Trix?" he said. "I'm sorry. I've been an ass about—about a lot of it. I guess this place has screwed with my head more than I realized."

The regret in his voice brought me straight to him. I hugged him like I'd tried to the night before, and this time he welcomed the embrace, squeezing me tight. The tart copper smell of him filled my nose, and the muscles in his arms flexed against my back, holding me and sheltering me at once like he always had.

The words spilled out without any thought at all. "It was mostly my fault. My head hasn't really been on straight either. I never wanted to argue with you at all. We should be standing up to Roseborne together."

"We will. We'll show them, yeah? All of those pricks."

"Yeah." I swallowed thickly, my grip on him tightening. The decision didn't feel so difficult now. "Cade, before any of that, I really need to tell you, about Sylvie—"

"Hey." He stroked his hand over my hair. "We've both made our mistakes. It was a shitty thing, but I know you did it because of how much you care about me. I can't say I wouldn't have done something similar if I felt like I was losing you. I know you didn't want to hurt *me*. So there's nothing to talk about. Okay?"

He already knew. He knew and he wasn't holding it against me, and so much gratitude welled up inside me that it burned at the back of my eyes. I tipped my head against his shoulder and just soaked in his presence for a little longer.

But we didn't have much time. I couldn't let my relief overwhelm everything else. I eased back so I could look at him. "I think I've been getting somewhere. I've found out some things about the school and the staff, and I've been working on ways to get more info, maybe totally cut off the staff's source of power."

"That's amazing, Trix." Cade beamed at me. "And I bet they figured you didn't stand a chance."

"I haven't been able to work everything out," I added quickly. "But we've put quite a few pieces together. It seems like the professors and the dean are—"

My voice faltered at the stiffening of Cade's expression. He cocked his head, his hand coming up to rest against the side of my face. "We?"

"Well, I— You know a few of the other students have been helping me. They've been here longer—they've seen more than I have."

His gaze searched mine, a shadow darkening his gray eyes. "They haven't been *just* helping you, have they." It wasn't a question.

My face heated despite my best efforts to control my reaction. "What do you mean?"

He grimaced. "It's my fault. I didn't handle things well, I wasn't patient enough with you, so of course you were tempted. I'm not going to blame you for ignoring your instincts. And they've been stuck here all this time, like you said—why wouldn't they want to get off with the new girl?"

It was true that my first instinct had been to keep my distance from all three of the guys—to be wary of their motives. But— "I don't think it's like that."

"Oh, Baby Bea. Most of the time you're tough as nails, but every now and then you're too sweet for your own good. Don't you think that's exactly why they swooped in on you? They could tell you have your issues, that you're not the girlfriend type, and they wanted to prove they could score with you anyway. They probably even figured it'd be easier with the way this place has jerked you around. And I had to go playing into that." He let out a frustrated huff.

I didn't know what to say. "They haven't done anything to hurt me," I started, but even as the words came out, I knew that wasn't entirely true. Jenson had taken plenty of jabs at me before. Elias had tried to freeze me out.

Cade spoke into my hesitation. "You know it's true. You're smart enough. So they misled you—you've just got to get those shields up now. They don't really know you, not all of you, not even most of you. They'd never get who you've had to be, the things you let happen, the things you've done. What do you really think would happen if you tried to have some kind of honest relationship with them?"

The question echoed all the doubts that had been creeping through me since I'd started letting the other guys in. Cade should know, shouldn't he? He'd seen the worst of me—he knew just how bad it was. And out there in the real world, no other guy had ever wanted to deal with my damaged history. Why would these three be any different?

I'd given them an escape, something to distract themselves, maybe even a little hope, just like they'd given me. It wasn't going to last. I *had* known that all along, hadn't I?

"You're right," I said quietly. "I wasn't letting myself really think about it. I just wanted— It was stupid, and kind of selfish too."

"You're allowed to be selfish," Cade said. "I love that part of you as much as every other. It just kills me thinking about you spending all that time with them, letting them think they've won, when I'm stuck out here like a fucking animal. It kills me even more *seeing* it." His hands dropped to his sides, clenching.

Shit. When had he seen me with any of the guys? We had mostly spent time together outside the school—Elias and I had been kissing at the edge of these woods just a few days ago. For all I knew Cade had ventured as far as the other side of campus when I'd hooked up with Jenson and Ryo.

My cheeks flared even hotter than before. "I'm sorry. I

wasn't thinking. I should have stopped it sooner anyway." The really stupid thing was how I'd let myself be fooled into buying into the theoretical romance of it, when I'd known all along how much I was holding back. "I think I've almost finished what I need to do anyway." The work I'd done on my basement passage tonight—pausing between every few taps of the hammer to listen for approaching staff—had gotten me so deep into the wall I *had* to be no more than a day or two away from breaking through.

"Don't change anything on my account," Cade said. "I just want to know you're looking after yourself. I can't protect you when I—"

He flinched, a tremor shaking his body. I grabbed his hand before he could pull away like he did every time the transformation came over him.

"You're protecting me right now by making me face up to what's really going on," I said. "That matters a lot."

He gave me a pained smile. "I know you'll do the right thing, Trix." Another shiver wracked his body, and he stumbled backward. "I'll be looking out for you as well as I can."

I watched his form fade into the thicker shadows, my stomach twisting into a knot. I had to look out for myself too, and that meant no more giving into delusional fantasies about who would really think I was worth the time of day.

I told myself it would be simple. A clean break, with no one really hurt—the best outcome for all of us.

Apparently I'd gotten better at lying to myself than even Cade had guessed.

As I picked up a plate with a runny omelet at the front of the cafeteria, Ryo ambled over to join me. My heart immediately flipflopped at the affection in his bright eyes.

I steeled myself. *Remember that he'd never look at you that way if he really knew you, Trix.* And why should he? I didn't need to put myself through that disappointment. I didn't need to see how disappointed *he'd* be. I was sparing both of us.

"They've really outdone themselves this time," he said in an amused tone, picking up a plate of his own. "Where should we grab a seat?"

There is no "we." There never really was.

"You should find someone else to sit with," I said.

Ryo blinked at me, only confused, not yet understanding. "Is everything okay, Trix?"

Everything was fine. I'd gotten my head on straight, stopped letting myself get distracted by the scraps of tenderness and desire that shouldn't have tempted me in the first place.

"No problems here," I said in the same even voice as before. "I've just been doing some thinking, and I've decided it's better if we only talk when we have real news to pass on. The work we've been doing—that's what really matters. What we should be focused on."

The furrow in his forehead dug deeper. "And you've been focused on it plenty. There's nothing wrong with taking some time for yourself in the moments in between."

There is if it's all based on a lie.

I held his gaze steadily. "This is what I want. And hopefully this whole situation will be over soon, and then it won't matter anymore."

The confusion in Ryo's expression was bleeding away into concern and a little hurt. "Trix, if something's happened—if I said or did something that made you think—"

Oh, God, I couldn't stand here listening to him trying to make this up to me as if I were some kind of innocent victim.

"It's got nothing to do with that," I interrupted. "This just makes everything simpler for all of us."

Before he could protest anymore, I fled out the door, taking my omelet with me.

I didn't trust Ryo not to follow me into the hall, so I went right through the front entrance and made my way over to the pool and my pathetic attempt at a garden. The first bite of the omelet left a faintly bitter aftertaste on my tongue. I forced it all down anyway, because I wasn't going to let myself waste away from literal starvation here.

When I looked up, it was immediately clear that I hadn't gone far enough. Not just Ryo but Jenson and Elias too were striding across the lawn toward me. Ryo must have gathered the troops.

Taking off on them didn't seem likely to work. I stood there waiting for them, my spine going rigid. The dark stretch of the campus woods filled the edge of my vision.

Cade could be prowling along the edges of the forest right now—he might see this confrontation. What would he make of it?

Why did they have to make everything so complicated? As soon as I'd found my brother, my path forward should have been obvious.

The guys stopped a few feet from where I stood, forming a semi-circle around me. Jenson was frowning, and Elias was studying me with his dark eyes. I wrapped one arm across my torso to steady myself.

"What's going on, Trix?" Jenson asked.

"I've just changed my mind about how I want things to be between me and all of you," I said. "Is it really that big of a deal? Can't you just accept it and move on?"

"Of course we will if that's how you feel," Ryo said. "We just want to be sure—with the way things are around here—if something else is going on that you're afraid to talk about or you think we'll get in trouble because of it, I hope you know we're still here, and we don't care about trouble. If there's any way you can tell us, we'll listen."

They wouldn't like what they'd hear—that was for sure. I shook my head, tossing my hair back over my shoulder. "There's nothing more to it. This is just me telling you to back off. We don't have to be friends or—or anything else for us to keep figuring out how to get the hell out of this place."

Elias's expression had turned increasingly thoughtful in a way that pricked at my skin. "No, we don't. I hope we haven't given you any reason to believe we *expect* you to offer more than that."

"I've got to say I'm starting to feel that way considering how determined you are to badger me about the decision." I shifted my weight uneasily, my mind lingering on Cade's form possibly looking on from the shadows between the trees. "Was that really what all your help was about in the first place—a way to make nice in the hopes you'd get into my pants?"

Jenson outright flinched, and Ryo's face grayed. "You know that was never what we—"

"I don't know anything," I shot back. If giving it to them straight wouldn't do the trick, then I'd just have to shove them away, even if that tactic sent an ache through my gut. "Other than I'm telling you to back off and none of you seem capable of listening to me. Just based on that, it looks like you care a lot more about what you want than what I do."

"Trix," Jenson started, his voice rough.

Elias held up his hand. Even out here when it was just the four of us, he still had that authoritative air that'd made him believable as a teacher.

"I think Beatrix is being very clear," he said. "She wants space—we should give that to her." He held my gaze. "I'm sorry if we got too pushy. We were worried about you, but I trust that you can let us know if you need anything from us after all."

"Are we really going to just—" Jenson tried again, and cut himself off at a sharp look from the brawnier guy. He scowled, but when Elias gestured, he turned to tramp with him and Ryo back toward the school.

My shoulders came down by fractions of inches as the

distance between us grew. The ache in my gut expanded too. That sense of loss was only longing for a fantasy that had always been ephemeral, though. The fact that it hurt now was all the more reason I shouldn't have let it go on even this long.

I couldn't hang back here for the rest of the morning. I had laundry duty after breakfast. Once the guys had plenty of time to get a head start on me, I marched back inside, dropped my plate off in the kitchen, and went down to the cool cement room I'd become increasingly familiar with over the past week.

I was the first person on this shift to arrive. I guessed I should go grab the bins of dirty linens to start hauling them down. But as I turned to leave again, a punch of rose scent hit my nose.

Smelling roses wasn't at all unusual on its own, but I'd never caught a whiff that thick down here before. I dragged in another breath, and the smell congealed in my lungs. A shiver ran down my back.

This didn't feel right.

Without another thought, my feet carried me toward the dryer I'd been using. I braced my hands on its cool side and peered behind it.

The bottom of my stomach dropped out. I stared, swiped at my eyes, and stared some more, getting queasier by the second.

The passage I'd spent so many nights chiseling away at, the one that I'd been sure had almost broken through to the secret space on the other side... no longer existed. The wall was the same solid, dimpled but otherwise unmarked concrete surface it'd been when I'd first started.

The hole hadn't even been filled in, at least not by any method I could imagine. It'd simply vanished as if it'd never been there in the first place.

CHAPTER TWENTY-FOUR

Trix

The sound of voices entering the basement broke me from my shock. Before the other students on laundry duty could reach the room, I ducked down and peered under the dryer.

As I'd already guessed, my tools had vanished too. Somehow I doubted they'd reappear back in the maintenance shed. They were gone for good.

I straightened up with a chill spreading through my abdomen. The staff must have found out, whether they knew I was the one who'd carved that passage or not. Who else could have sealed the hole over so completely? Had they picked up on my activities last night and just decided not to interrupt me in the moment? Had one of the students noticed and tattled on me?

The others came in hauling a couple of laundry baskets, and I got to work stuffing the sheets and pillowcases into the washing machines on autopilot. My mind kept whirring away.

Violet and her roommates had seemed suspicious about me being down here the other day. Maybe one of them had poked around some more. None of them had acted happy about the fact that I might be working against the school's interests somehow.

What had Violet said when I'd talked to her later that day? Something about taking a stand of her own—about making sure the staff wouldn't hurt her anymore. She'd claimed that she felt bad about criticizing me... but maybe she'd just been covering her tracks. I didn't have any reason to think she liked me all that much. She could have gone to the staff and offered to make a deal: her information in exchange for them backing off on her.

I stewed on the possibilities through the rest of laundry duty, the physical labor only sharpening my thoughts. While I carried bins of clean linens back upstairs to their homes, I scanned the halls and rooms I passed for that cloud of dark hair and the partly scarred face beneath.

Was Violet a good enough liar that she'd be able to blow off a confrontation? I was going to find out—because I needed to know exactly what she'd told them, if anything.

I spotted her on my final trek through the school building. When I came out of the girls' bathroom after restocking the towel shelves, my former roommate was just coming out of the Tolerance classroom with several other students, all of them pale and a little unsteady on their feet. My stomach turned with the memory of my own experiences with Professor Marsden's "teaching" methods.

Maybe I could learn something just by observing before I took this to a direct confrontation. I meandered after Violet, keeping a careful distance. She headed down the stairs to the first floor and stepped into the sitting room. I went around the other side of the stairs by the portraits and watched her through the rungs of the banister.

All she did was go to the front window and stand there, gazing toward the gate. Her hands opened and clenched at her sides. With a jerk of her body, she strode to the front door and charged outside.

Where the hell was she going like that? I hustled to the door and eased it open.

Violet had already crossed most of the lawn between the school building at the wall to the left of the gate, her steps brisk. Something glinted in her hand. An uneasy tension coiled around my gut.

I slipped outside, hesitated for a moment, and then followed her once she'd marched into the shelter of the scattered trees at the north end of campus. Whatever she was up to, it didn't seem to have anything to do with the staff. That didn't mean it was a good thing, though. The rigid defiance in her posture set off alarm bells I couldn't ignore.

I skirted the wall, heading in the same direction Violet had gone. She'd gotten far enough ahead of me in the sparse forest that I couldn't make her out anymore. A fresh wave of uneasiness prickled over me. I sped up my pace until I was just shy of jogging.

Her form came into view up ahead, right by the wall. A pair of steel scissors yawned open in her hands—around the stem of a rose. *Her* rose, if I remembered from my past explorations right. My pulse stuttered, and I threw myself forward.

"Violet!"

She glanced up at me without changing her grip on the scissors. Her eyes shone stark and wild. "I'm not letting them call the shots anymore," she said. "It's my fucking life, and I decide what happens to it."

Before I could reach her, she slammed the scissors' blades closed.

The rose's stem was tough, and the scissors, which I guessed she'd stolen from the kitchen at some point, weren't the sharpest ever. They sliced most but not all the way through. The rose drooped forward, hanging by a sliver—and Violet shuddered so violently the scissors fell from her hands. She staggered back and crumpled over.

"No!" I dashed the rest of the way to her and dropped to my knees at her side. Her breath came slow and shallow, but her jaw hung limp, and she didn't rouse when I shook her shoulder.

Her rose was still alive, but only barely. It wasn't going to stay alive like that. Had she *meant* to commit this disjointed sort of suicide, or had she been hoping that if she severed the thing connecting her to the school, she'd be able to go free?

Even if I'd known for sure she'd wanted to die, I didn't

think I could have left her and done nothing. Not knowing—I had to try to save her. I looked up at the rose, sorting through all the gardening knowledge I'd accumulated over the years.

I'd taken a few roses from the Monroes' bush to start fresh plants I'd managed to sell for a little cash. I didn't have the gardening chemicals I'd used to help that along here, but I could make full use of what I did have.

I ran back to the shed against the side of the school and fumbled through the shelves for a few things that might help: gardening shears, a glass jar I emptied several rusty nails out of, a little spade. Then I sprinted back to the spot where Violet had fallen as quickly as I could.

My heart beat at the base of my throat as I snipped the rose the rest of the way off the bush. Violet didn't stir, but her chest kept its faint rise and fall. The rose in my hand still held most of its bloom, only a little brown along the edges of the petals. Now I had to make sure it stayed that way. I had no idea how much time I had until the connection between it and my former roommate destroyed them both.

It wasn't quite as long a cutting as I'd have wanted, but I'd have to make do. Grateful for the experience that guided my shaky hands, I snipped the lowest leaves off the stem and used one edge of the shears to carve a small slit at the bottom. Then I dug into the earth just in front of the larger bush, stirring up the soil. It was still moist from the recent rain—at least that worked in my favor.

Carefully, I eased the stem halfway down into the earth and patted the dirt firm around it to hold it up. The leaves trembled as I eased the jar over the part aboveground to hold in the moisture and protect it from wandering animals. There. I sat back on my heels, my breath rushing out of me.

My approach might not be good enough for new roots to sprout. I'd never tried without a concoction meant to stimulate that growth. But leaving the bloom dangling from the bush would have meant certain, swift death. I just wished there was more I could do.

Violet stirred, her eyelids fluttering. With the unmarked side of her face against the ground and only the scars showing, she looked even more wounded than usual.

"Violet?" I said tentatively.

Her eyelids twitched again. She wheezed, but the breath was a little steadier than the ones before. Her hand fumbled across the weedy ground in front of her. I scooted over to grasp it.

"Hey. Are you awake? Can you talk to me?"

She managed to peer up at me. Her lips jerked at a painful angle. Her whole body trembled as her fingers tightened around mine.

"I replanted it," I said, braced for anger at my admission. "Your rose—so that it can keep growing. I'm not sure—if it dies, then you—"

She closed her eyes for a second and seemed to gird herself. "Okay," she said in a rasp of a voice. "Fuck."

She didn't sound as if she wanted to be dead right now. A hint of relief trickled through me, mostly overshadowed by my fear that I hadn't actually saved her, only prolonged a drawn-out demise. I glanced toward the school. I couldn't leave her lying here for who knew how long until she—maybe—got her strength back.

"If you can move a little, I can help you get back to the school so you can recover somewhere more comfortable," I said. "Or I can go get help."

Her head gave a sharp shake before I'd quite finished that second sentence. Violet was probably pissed off enough that she had even one spectator to her disastrous stunt. Her body swayed, stiffened, and then lurched upright far enough that I could leverage her weight against mine. I stood slowly, bringing her with me, her arm clamped across my shoulders.

"Here we go," I said, willing myself not to tense up at having another person I wasn't even sure I liked that much clinging so closely to me.

She could plant her feet well enough to keep herself upright, but I more dragged her than supported her walking through the trees and across the lawn. By the time we made it to the school, my own breath was coming short, my shoulders aching from supporting so much of her weight. We staggered up the steps and into the sitting room.

The thought of attempting the larger staircases to get Violet up to the dorm made me wince. I helped her onto the sofa instead. She lay down and curled up with her face to the padded back of the seat. No word of thanks. She hadn't said anything other than those first two words when I'd told her what was going on.

I couldn't say I regretted intervening, though.

Would the staff realize what I'd done just now—that I

knew about the roses and their significance, that I'd meddled with that one? Between that and the discovered passage in the basement, how much longer did I have before they decided to use their power to send me back to the beginning of my journey here again?

Would I remember what I'd already been through the next time, or would that fade away like it had all the other times before?

Maybe if I came up with some kind of story to redirect them before they put all the pieces together, I could buy myself a little more time.

I hurried up to the second-floor classrooms, but the Composition room was empty. Out of all the professors, Hubert was my best chance at getting any kind of sympathy. I'd made at least a little progress warming her up to me. I wavered and then headed back downstairs to the hall with the staff offices.

Did the professors actually live in their rooms when they didn't need to be directing students here, or did they vanish to some supernatural realm? I had no idea, but Hubert opened the door a few seconds after my knock. Her hair was piled in its usual heap on top of her head, her gaze as piercing as ever.

"Yes, Miss Corbyn?" she said. Her voice sounded snippier than the last couple of times we'd talked. Because I'd interrupted something or because she knew I'd been working against the staff after all?

"Something's happened to one of the students," I said. "I'm not sure what to do."

At a regular school, I'd imagine a teacher hearing that

would have hustled right out to take in the situation. Instead, Professor Hubert motioned me inside with an only partly stifled sigh. "Why don't you explain?"

The room I found on the other side definitely wasn't the sort of space I could picture a person living in. It was small and stuffy, with bookcases along one wall and a wooden desk with a single chair on the far side. Hubert didn't bother to sit down, just leaned against the front of her desk, so I had nothing to do but stand awkwardly in front of her.

"I found Violet down by the wall around campus," I said, letting the words spill out urgently so any holes in my story would sound more like I was flustered than I was leaving things out. "She'd fainted or something—she seemed really weak. I don't even know what she was doing out there. It looked like she was trying to replant one of the roses off the bush?"

Hubert regarded me, coolly contemplative. "And you left her there?"

"No," I said. "I managed to wake her up a little and help her get back to the school. She's resting in the sitting room right now. But I don't know if she's sick or something. It looks pretty serious. Maybe she should see an actual doctor?"

For a moment, silence hung between us. Hubert's eyes had widened slightly. "Have you gotten particularly close with Miss Droz?" she asked. "You seem very invested in her well-being."

I blinked at her. "If I see someone who's obviously in trouble, of course I'm going to try to help."

"Perhaps you wouldn't feel that way if you knew how much trouble that girl brought on others of her own volition."

Was she seriously suggesting that I should have left Violet to die because of her past? Well, yeah, that actually did seem to fit with the staff's usual attitudes.

I folded my arms over my chest. "I know about the bomb. She told me. It was a shitty thing to do, but that doesn't mean I want to see her suffering. Anyway, that's not the point. Are you going to make sure she's okay or what?"

The professor's gaze had slid away from me. She was looking toward the bookshelves, which held a few framed photographs in front of the rows of books. A couple of them black and white, the other two sepia toned—scenes from around the school, I realized when I studied them. They would have fit in with the pictures in the yearbook I'd found, except I didn't recognize any of them from those pages.

The same boy featured in three of them. The malnourished-looking boy with the tufts of pale hair who was missing from the portraits: Winston Baker. In one, he stood at the edge of the frame, looking toward students sprawled around the swimming pool. In another, he and a different boy braced themselves on the badminton court, their expressions grim. In the third, he was sitting at a cafeteria table, with—

"Love or selfishness," Professor Hubert murmured, so quietly I barely made out the words, her eyes still fixed on the photographs. "Has that always been the key?"

I was still looking at the picture of the boy in the cafeteria. Looking, and then tumbling through my mind into the vague impression of a seat, chatter carrying around me, a meaty smell hanging in the air. My ribs hurt —someone had kicked me in them—and my fingers clenched around…

Around a gold pocket watch etched with a distinctive pattern of whorls and lines that came together into a tree.

The sight, momentarily crystal clear, jolted me back to the present. The watch was right there in the photograph, half hidden by the boy's hand, but the etching on it was visible enough for me to know it was the same as on my mother's watch. The one she'd said had come from her grandfather. How—why—?

Winston Baker had the same watch as my great-grandfather. It was Winston Baker's memories I'd been slipping into. Winston Baker, whose portrait no longer got painted to be hung in Roseborne's front hall.

Icy fingers raced over my skin. I blurted out the question before I could think better of it. "Why are there only seven portraits in the hall now?"

Hubert's gaze snapped back to me. "Pardon me?"

I fumbled with my words. "In the hall by the dean's office. There are those painted portraits—someone told me there's a contest every year. But there's a spot where it looks like there used to be another one hanging and nothing's there now. Why was one of them taken down?"

The professor's brow knit. My abrupt change in subject had to have thrown her. But I might get a more honest answer because of that.

"That place of honor was abandoned," she said stiffly. "Given up, never returned—not really."

With that disjointed statement, her expression took on the weirdly analytical vibe I'd seen before, as if she were trying to discern something beneath my face.

As if she were looking for someone else there.

My heart skittered. I groped for something else to say. But Hubert was already motioning toward the door. "I think that's enough of a talk. I'll see that Miss Droz is looked after. Don't worry yourself about it."

I stepped out of her office in a daze. As the door clicked shut behind me, I stared at the wall across from me without really seeing it.

Sometime around 1927, eight students had done something that had transformed Roseborne forever. One of them had abandoned the school and never returned. That one had a pocket watch I knew and whose memories were seeping into my head.

Me, the one person who'd remembered someone Roseborne had swallowed up despite the staff's obvious powers—the one person they hadn't been able to make stay away and instead had locked into this bizarre cycle of repeating arrivals. I could be more connected to this place than any other student had ever been.

What other powers might *I* have that I hadn't stumbled on yet?

CHAPTER TWENTY-FIVE

Trix

I didn't feel all that powerful as I waited in the hall outside the math classroom. The thought of looking Elias in the face after the way I'd cast off him and the other two guys this morning made me queasy. But I had to talk to *someone*, and out of my available options, Elias was the one I trusted most to keep a clear head and give me his honest take on the situation.

If there was something horrifying about my discovery, he'd show it. If he could think of anything I could do that would make the situation better, he'd tell me, even if it'd be hard. I thought I could count on that.

The door opened, and the students drifted out. I stayed where I was. A couple of minutes after the last of them had wandered away, Elias himself emerged, looking vaguely harried but glad to be done. He stopped in his tracks when he saw me, his chin lifting and his shoulders pushing back to give him an even more professional appearance in the suit he filled out so well.

"Beatrix," he said, and left me to decide where to go from there.

"Elias." I resisted the urge to nibble at my lip. "Something's come up that I was hoping I could talk through with you. About, ah, the schoolwork. Do you have a moment?"

I could tell from his expression that he understood what kind of "schoolwork" I meant. He nodded and motioned for me to walk with him. As always when we were inside the school, he kept a studied distance from me on the way down the stairs.

We stepped outside into the dim sunlight and cool air beneath the clouded sky. My feet moved toward the northern section of wall instinctively, even though it wasn't likely I'd be able to tell how well my planting of Violet's rose was working just yet.

Elias walked alongside me in silence, giving me the space to decide how and when I began. Somehow that only made me feel more ill. I swiped my hand across my mouth.

"This doesn't change what I said this morning. It isn't personal. You and the other guys—you're still the ones who have the best handle on what's going on at Roseborne and what I've figured out so far."

"Understood," Elias said quietly. "Do you want to tell me what 'came up' today?"

The truth was, not really. A large part of me was dreading finding out how he'd look at me, talk to me, if he agreed with the conclusions I'd drawn. But why the hell had I brought him out here if I wasn't going to lay it out and see whether I'd just gone bonkers?

"It's big," I said, grappling with where to start. "I think it explains why I was able to remember Cade and this place to begin with, and why the staff don't believe they can simply kick me out and keep me from causing more problems for them. Why I've been having those weird memories that aren't mine. All of it. But it's probably going to sound kind of crazy."

"Why don't you start from the beginning, and we'll see where it gets us." Elias shot me a careful smile. "I promise I won't sugarcoat my opinion on your sanity."

"That's why I came to you." I dragged in a breath. "Okay. First, you need to know that my mother had this pocket watch—gold, on a chain, with an interesting etching on the case. I've never seen another one like it. And it was weird, really, that she held onto it at all, when it was obviously an antique and she and my dad rarely held on to anything they could cash in to buy drugs for more than a week or two. She said it was her grandfather's, but she didn't care much about family otherwise."

"I can see why you'd remember it, then," Elias said.

"Yeah. And today, I went to talk to Professor Hubert in her office. She has some photos up from what's got to be the same era at Roseborne as the yearbook. Most of them had the eighth guy from the art room photos in them, the one no one makes a portrait of anymore."

"Winston."

Of course he'd remember the name after only discussing it once.

"Yeah, and in one of the photos… he was holding a pocket watch. A pocket watch that looked exactly like the one my mom had. And when I looked at the photograph, another of those memories hit me, like I fell right into that moment—inside his head. It could be all the weird memories that have come over me were his. I tried to ask Professor Hubert about the eighth portrait, and all she said was a bit of vague stuff about him abandoning Roseborne and not coming back."

When I glanced at Elias to see what he made of that, he was gazing into the distance, his brow knit. "I have noticed over the years that there are times when one or another of the professors won't have any classes for a week or two. I don't have any proof, because the new students show up at random times, but I've wondered if they leave to go looking for new targets. I'm not sure how they'd find us otherwise. That theory makes even more sense if she's basically confirming that they *can* leave, and they have some choice about whether they come back."

"But they've always come back except Winston, whenever he left the last time." That wasn't the main point I'd expected Elias to focus on, though. My fingers curled into my palms.

He hadn't totally missed my train of thought. He glanced over at me, his hand twitching as if he'd been going to reach for mine and stopped himself. "You're thinking because of the watch and the memories—and the fact that you made it here at all—that after he left, he might have started a family. That whatever the staff became to give them all this power, they're still human enough to have kids. And he was your mother's grandfather, your great-grandfather."

He didn't sound disgusted by the thought. My next breath came a little easier. "The pieces seem to fit. A little bit of his affinity with the college could have passed on to me, made it so I'm partly immune to their magic. Obviously the staff still here are way stronger than I am, since they're completely... whatever they are, and I'm only an eighth or something, but it was enough to make a difference."

Whatever they were, whatever monstrous energy they'd let take them over, it ran through my veins too, even if diluted. I rubbed my arms, suppressing a shiver. The breeze murmured through the leaves of the trees we'd passed between and licked over me, tugging at the sleeves of my shirt and the hem of my skirt. I wished I'd brought my leather jacket for this walk.

"I'm not sure if we'd ever be able to confirm it for sure," Elias said. "It could be that this Winston guy gave his watch to your actual grandfather, and a little magic transferred with it. I'd say it's pretty clear there's some connection, though."

"Some of the energy that keeps this place running is inside me." My mouth twisted. "Some of that awfulness."

"Hey." Elias touched my arm lightly to stop me. He looked down at me, his dark eyes solemn. "You can't blame yourself for anything that happens here. Whoever Winston was to you, *he* abandoned this place. Apparently he didn't like how things were going either. And whatever powers you've got in you, you've been using them to try to help us, not the staff. You're nothing like them."

Other than I could be cruel and vindictive when I had enough reason to be. I ducked my head. "I don't think that's totally true. I've done awful things, even if you haven't had to see them. There've been times when I hardly felt like I could control myself. I doubt you of all people would give that a pass."

To my surprise, Elias laughed. "Are you kidding me? Trix, do you have any idea—I love that you're unpredictable, that sometimes you say what you're thinking without worrying about the consequences, that you're not afraid to let loose—it's something I never really learned. If being that way led to some awful situations too... well, as far as I'm concerned, that's a fair trade-off. Being a control freak didn't stop me from wreaking havoc on a whole lot of people."

"It's easy to say—"

"I'm not just saying it." He hesitated and then touched my shoulder, letting his hand linger there. "What do you remember about the first time we really got to know each other?"

Those glimpses of the more distant past slipped through my mind again. Laughter, the wind in my hair, his hands hot against my body, a rush of exhilaration. Words I'd spoken rose up in the back of my head. *Have you seriously never climbed a tree in your whole life? We need to fix that.*

My gaze lifted to the scattered trees around you. "I got you to go tree-climbing?"

He smiled sheepishly. "With a certain amount of badgering. And I felt pretty ridiculous at first. But ridiculous and then free, like I'm not sure I ever have before."

An impulse hit me—one of those unpredictable urges Elias had just said he loved. My body balked for a second with the thought of Cade, of whether he might somehow be watching even now... But there was no sign of that hunched, coarse-furred beast I'd encountered in the southern woods anywhere around us.

And I needed to figure out where I really stood with Elias—with all the guys—for myself too, didn't I? I wouldn't really trust my judgement unless I'd made it for myself.

"What are you waiting for, then?" I said to Elias, already taking off toward the nearest tree with low enough branches. "You've already practiced once. Let's see who can get higher faster."

Elias's next laugh dissolved into a hasty breath as he jogged after me. He gripped the branches of a maple next to mine and hauled himself onto the lowest one with a flexing of his shoulders that I couldn't help admiring. I scrambled farther up, not letting myself think too hard about where I set my hands or feet, the ground falling away beneath me.

When I looked over at Elias again, he'd climbed nearly as high up as I had. He caught my eye with a rueful shake of his head, but he was beaming at the same time.

Grinning with so much joy that the sight knocked the breath out of me.

He hadn't been kidding or lying. He loved this—he loved that I'd gotten him to do it. He liked *me* even with my reckless side.

A tingle shot through me, so potent I could almost taste electricity on my tongue. Abruptly, I was sure that right now, in this moment, not one member of Roseborne's staff could have found me on campus. The power that had shielded me before was wrapping around me again.

But this—this didn't really prove anything about Elias. This was just fun. The worst possible danger was a short fall that wasn't all that likely considering those muscles of his. Would he still think I was so great if I challenged him in ways that could really screw him over?

Lust and a different sort of hunger—to be sure, to test my power and his affection—swelled inside me. I leapt down a few branches and then sprang straight to the ground, the landing jolting through my legs.

"Come with me," I said. "We can let loose way more than this."

Elias raised his eyebrows, but he clambered down after me. I caught his hand briefly with a little tug and set off for the school building.

When we made it inside, I headed straight up the stairs without looking back at him. The rasp of his shoes against the floor right behind me set off little sparks of anticipation through my chest—and lower.

Was this stupid? Maybe. Maybe I should have steered

clear of the guys like I'd planned to. But I was more than just the girl I'd thought I was this morning. He couldn't hurt me, not if I didn't let him.

The question was, how much was he willing to risk me hurting *him*?

I pushed past the door to the math classroom. When Elias had come in after me, I twisted the lock on the knob. With my pulse thrumming all through my body, I nudged him toward his desk and hopped up on its edge, shoving the stack of textbooks to the side. Then I held out my hand to him.

"Fuck me," I said. "Right here, right now."

Elias's pupils dilated with desire. Seeing his longing written all over his face made me want him even more. His voice came out hoarse. "Trix, are you sure—"

"I think I can stop the staff from realizing what we're doing," I said. "But I can't promise that absolutely. I don't know how they'll react if they catch on. It'd probably be worse for you than for me."

He might hate me for even asking him to take that risk. That was fine. Then I'd know.

Elias hesitated for just a second longer. Then he stepped up to me and tipped my face to meet his lips.

His mouth claimed mine, all searing passion, so intense I started to melt right there. My hands fisted the fabric of his shirt and jerked it free from his slacks. When I pushed at his suit jacket, he shed it from one arm and then the other, as if he couldn't bear to let go of my face completely. I ran my hands up under his shirt, tracing the lines of taut muscle there, and he hummed approvingly in the middle of our next kiss.

It was more of a risk, shedding clothes. More when I unbuttoned his shirt. He didn't make a move to stop me, though. He just kept devouring my mouth, his tongue slicking over mine so teasingly I gasped as I explored every solid plane of his brawny body. How dare he keep this much deliciousness so tightly under wraps.

He wanted me. Even when it was dangerous, even when I'd shown I was willing to lead him straight toward that danger. He thought having this was worth whatever the consequences might be.

Maybe that would change if he knew everything, but for now, for this, that knowledge was enough.

I didn't have much patience to draw this out now that I had him so eager. He trailed one hand down my shoulder and under my shirt to caress my breast, and I reached for the button of his slacks. My gasp at the flick of his thumb over my nipple was echoed by his groan when my fingers grazed his erection. Fuck, he was big there too.

I was abruptly grateful for the skirt. While I freed his impressive cock from his slacks and boxers, all Elias had to do was slide his hands up under that length of plaid fabric and tug my leggings and panties down. As they dropped to my ankles, I spread my knees. He dipped his fingers between us to stroke my clit and then down over my opening.

The pulse of pleasure he summoned made me twice as desperate for release as before. A demanding growl slipped from my throat.

He chuckled with a stutter of breath and pulled me even closer to him, right to the edge of the desk. My ankles hooked behind him. He kissed me again, hard, as he thrust inside me.

The sudden heady friction sent a wave of bliss through me to the top of my head. I kissed him back and swayed to meet him. As he plunged in and out of me, his fingers gripping my thigh to hold me steady on the desk, the throb of need inside me only expanded. I soared higher and higher, my mouth colliding with his again, my hands charting every inch of his bared chest.

It felt *right*, like that burst of passion in the gazebo with Jenson and Ryo, like nothing had before. Was it possible I'd found something true with all three of these guys after all, no matter what Cade said?

My mind slipped back to Professor Hubert's comment about love or selfishness, and then spiraled away into a deeper haze of pleasure. Elias shifted his hand to tease over my clit as he sped up his thrusts, a sharper spike of bliss joining the rest, and I came apart against him, moaning and clenching and feeling him tumble into his own release a moment later.

If this counted as love, who the hell wouldn't choose it?

CHAPTER TWENTY-SIX

Elias

Trix sagged into me, her legs still wrapped around my hips. I held onto her as the aftershock of the orgasm washed through my body. Holy fuck, I didn't think I'd ever had one quite that intense.

Whatever she'd done, whatever power she had, no one had interrupted us. Thank God for that. I brushed my fingers over her hair, and she nestled a little more securely against me, but I could already feel a hint of tension starting to collect in her muscles, preparing to pull away.

No. Whatever had gotten into her today, whatever had changed her mind and brought us to this point, I wasn't sure I'd find a better chance to get through to her. She needed to know I wasn't in this just for my personal satisfaction—that her happiness meant more to me than my own. That she could turn to me no matter what.

I eased away from her just far enough to pull my slacks

back up and then help her squirm back into her leggings. As I rebuttoned my shirt, she slid off the desk, looking ready to leave. I paused and caught her arm.

"Come with me?" I said. "There are some things I think I should tell you that I haven't yet."

Trix considered me, the conflicted apprehension I'd seen on her face this morning creeping back in, but she stayed as I tugged on my suit jacket. I led her out of the math classroom and, to her obvious surprise, around the landing to the stairs to the guys' dorm. As I headed up, she balked.

"Is this really a good idea?" she said.

"It'll be fine. We've got a system. I'll show you."

I offered her a reassuring smile, and curiosity seemed to win her over. She followed me up.

As I'd expected, my bedroom was empty. No one generally hung out in the dorm during the day. I grabbed a sock from my under-bed chest and rested it over the outer door knob.

"We have a sign to let the other guys in the room know we need privacy for a while," I said. "There's a sort of unspoken agreement not to monopolize the room for more than an hour or so, but—people are going to want to hook up, even in a place like this."

Trix arched an eyebrow at me. "We did already get the hooking up part over with."

"I know. But my desk isn't exactly an ideal spot for an after hook-up chat. I want a lot more with you than just to get my dick wet, Trix."

I sat down on my bed. After a moment, Trix sank

down next to me. When I slipped my hand around her waist, she lay down with me, tucked close so we could both fit on the narrow bed, face to face. Her hand came to rest on the side of my chest.

I tucked a few stray strands of her bright hair behind her ear and hugged her close. It took a few minutes, but her body gradually relaxed into mine. Her fingers curled into the fabric of my jacket as if she wanted to hold me in place. As if I had any intention of going anywhere as long as she wanted me with her.

"Do you remember much about what I've told you before about my life outside Roseborne?" I asked, keeping my voice low.

"You told me last time about how focused you were on developing a business, getting ahead," she said. "That you screwed over people to give yourself a leg up. And I remember a few bits from before that... Your grandfather encouraged you a lot?"

"That's one way of putting it." I drew in a breath. This wasn't my favorite subject, what with the memories that had become increasingly uncomfortable the longer Roseborne had forced me to delve into my past, but it was better we started out by talking about me rather than about her. She needed to know how well I could understand, how I could read the signs—that I wasn't just speaking from a place of jealousy.

"My grandfather on my mother's side had one of those stories they point to when they talk about the American Dream," I said. "He moved here from Mexico with his family when he was a teenager, managed to excel in school and get scholarships, made connections with the right people and started his own business that started to take off when he was only in his twenties. He just kept building it and reinforcing his finances—I think he was always a little paranoid that the tide could turn and all he'd have left to rely on were his savings."

"That seems understandable," Trix said.

"Yeah. I can't blame him for that." I pressed a quick kiss to her forehead before continuing. "My mother was the only kid he and my grandmother ended up having, and he wanted even better things for her, but she had her own ideas... She ended up getting married pretty young to a guy from a blue collar family my grandfather didn't approve of at all. When I was four, she died giving birth to my sister. My grandparents stepped in, offered our father a chunk of money to hand over custody to them and stay out of our lives, and he... took it. I haven't seen him since."

My throat tightened. I only had hazy impressions left of either of my parents, but my father's abandonment stung deep down in my gut in a way I'd never been able to shake. He'd wanted the money more than he'd wanted his own children in his life.

Trix tucked her head closer to mine. "That's awful."

"Well, I guess it proved my grandparents were right about him. Anyway, my grandfather had very set ideas about how things should work. How we should behave. And he made his approval or disapproval very clear. He only ever let on that he cared about us, gave us any attention, if we showed off some kind of smarts or business sense. If we just acted like kids, he'd be cold and detached. It killed me when it seemed like I was disappointing him. So I worked my ass off, got the best grades I could, did everything I could think of around the house to show how industrious I was—anything to get a scrap of praise."

I heard Trix's grimace in her voice. "*That's* pretty awful too."

I nodded, my chin grazing her hair. "I'm sure he thought he was just molding my sister and I into the best people we could be. At the time, I didn't know anything else. I thought I only deserved any kind of affection if I'd earned it—I thought any time he withdrew from me, it was because there was something wrong with me and I just had to do better. And as I worked harder and harder, made it to the top of my class and impressed my first employers and all that... I started thinking about everyone around me the same way. What they'd earned compared to what I had. Whether I deserved things more than them. Why should anyone have something I wanted if I'd proven I was better than them? And that was when I became a real prick."

"Because your grandfather was a prick to you."

My chest still constricted hearing those words spoken out loud, even though I'd come to terms with that fact a while ago.

"I can't completely blame him," I said. "I still made my own choices—the responsibility for them is mostly mine. But having someone I cared about and relied on that much treat me that way, going hot and cold depending on how well I lived up to his very specific expectations, making me feel I was always walking a tightrope between keeping his approval and losing it… It messes a person up. It messes with your ability to figure out what you really want for yourself and who *you'd* really want to be. I can see now that he wasn't making me better or stronger, he was just making me more what suited his preferences. And that screwed up my internal compass so much that I made some horrible decisions."

Trix was silent for a long moment. Had the parallels started to occur to her? Finally, she said, "You told me someone died because of one of those decisions."

"Yeah." My jaw clenched before I managed to force out the words. "My sister ended up going in the opposite direction from me. Instead of working hard, she defied my grandparents whenever she could because she hated how they tried to control us. It drove me crazy that she made our lives so chaotic, that she wouldn't listen to them or me and see what she was doing wrong…

"When she was sixteen, she got sucked in by this older guy, almost thirty, and ended up moving in with him—I hardly saw her for months. I guess he liked it that way. She traded one dictator for another." I paused and propelled the rest of the words out. "She came to me a little after her seventeenth birthday with a big bruise on her cheek, looking terrified, asking if she could stay with me at my apartment. Saying she was scared of the guy and needed somewhere to hide after she left him. She didn't think our grandparents would take her back in."

"What did you say?" Trix asked as I grappled with the

next words. Her soft tone suggested she already suspected it.

"I told her she'd made her own bed and if she didn't like it, she had to fix it herself, not come begging for help from someone who'd made better choices. I said if she was that worried, she should go to our grandparents and show how sorry she was so she'd deserve their forgiveness. And then I shut the door on her." I closed my eyes. "She went back to him instead. A week later, he flew off the handle and stabbed her with a kitchen knife. The neighbors called the cops, but she'd already bled out when they got there."

"*He's* the one who killed her," Trix said.

"Yeah, but I knew he might. She was my *sister*. I should have cared more about protecting her than teaching her some stupid lesson. And it wasn't even for myself. Part of me wanted to help her, hated seeing her like that. But another part of me kept hearing my grandfather's voice in the back of my head, kept picturing the way he'd react if he found out I'd supported her mistakes."

"I guess it wasn't too long after that you ended up here?"

"The same month. I got a letter offering this exclusive advanced business specialization—I should have known it was bullshit. But they probably put some kind of persuasive power into it to make the offer sound like something you can't refuse."

"Cade went on about what an amazing opportunity it was, even though he hadn't been all that interested in college before." Trix gripped my jacket harder, tugging it toward her as if it could encompass us both. As if she could take shelter beneath it from everything waiting for us beyond this bed. "Why did you want to tell me all this now?"

I had to tread carefully here. "Because the way you've reacted in certain situations, things that you've said… It reminds me of how I felt sometimes back then. Like I was being pulled in two different directions, and I was so scared of making the 'wrong' decision and losing the person who'd given me so much."

Trix pressed her face to my chest. "It's not like he's trying to force me into anything when he gets into those moods," she mumbled, so quiet the words were almost lost in my shirt. "He just cares so much he can't help how he reacts."

I wasn't so sure about that from what I'd seen, but I could easily believe *she* believed it after the years she'd spent with no one else caring about her at all.

"I know my grandfather cared about me a lot too," I said. "I loved him. But that isn't enough. Someone can care about you and still mess with your head. No amount of loving someone will make them see they're hurting you if they're looking the other way." I hugged her tighter. "How many times have you done things you didn't want to because he made you feel like he'd pull away from you if you didn't?"

She winced, her back going rigid. "He's never said—he never *made* it like that."

"But the way he acted, you still felt like you had to worry about it."

"He didn't have to do anything for me in the first place."

"I know." I knew that justification all too well. The sense that if my grandfather got too fed up with me, I'd have no one at all. "Trix, I'm not trying to tell you that you shouldn't listen to him or be around him or anything like that. You know your brother a hell of a lot better than I do. I just—I *do* care about you too, and if there's any chance that talking about this helps you figure out what *you* really want, then I'll be happy. Even if what you really want is to back off from me and everyone else except him. That's up to you."

She inhaled shakily. "Okay. I'll think about it. It seems like everything's turned into such a shitstorm." She let those words trail off into the quiet of the room, and then she sat up next to me. A determined expression came over her face. "You know, it'd be a lot easier to figure this all out if we weren't stuck in this place with a bunch of psychos who are definitely out to make us miserable. I've got some kind of power—I'm going to use it."

As she got off the bed, I pushed myself upright. "What are you planning to do?"

She shot me a tight little smile. "I'm not totally sure yet—but I've got an axe to sharpen."

CHAPTER TWENTY-SEVEN

Trix

The rasp of the sharpening stone against the blade of the axe scraped the scattered emotions from my head. As I rested the axe's handle on my legs where I was sitting on the maintenance shed's cot, my mind narrowed down to nothing but the task in front of me—and the uneasy question my talk with Elias had raised.

It was my fault if I'd let Cade talk me into doing things I hadn't really wanted to, wasn't it? How was it fair to blame him when I'd made the decisions?

I'd like to think that, but it was far too easy to remember just a few nights ago when I'd made a different decision than the one he'd wanted. Why hadn't I said no or pulled back earlier when he'd tried to escalate the physical side of our relationship again? Why had I compromised on that position when I knew *I* didn't really want to see him as more than a brother and friend?

Because I'd known he'd withdraw, like he had. I'd known he'd be hurt and angry, that he'd distance himself from me, that he'd blame himself as if he'd done something wrong, and I hadn't wanted to face all that. I'd put his happiness, his desires, ahead of my own. Just like I had a hell of a lot of times over the years if I let myself stop to consider it.

I'd always told myself I owed him. That supporting him and being there beside him no matter what direction he took us in was the least I could do after he'd had my back for so long. Maybe that was still true.

But my thoughts kept returning to the last thing Elias had told me—that he wasn't going to tell me what I should do. That he thought my choices should be up to me, and if I got what I wanted, that was enough to make him happy.

So simple and yet so different from Cade the last time I'd talked to him—the way he'd warned me away from Elias and the others without reservation, *telling* me what I should want. What I could have. I couldn't look back on that conversation without seeing all the ways he'd steered me in one specific direction, discounting any possibility that I had choices beyond the one he expected me to take.

How had I not seen it before? Had he always pushed me that insistently? I didn't think so—but then, I'd never before pushed against him as firmly as I had the night I'd refused his advances. And I'd never had much to compare his behavior to. Until now, he'd been the only one I'd turned to in any way that mattered.

What was the truth, under all the confusion and the bullshit? I wanted Ryo and Jenson and Elias—all of them. I liked talking with them and the way they talked to me; I liked how they looked at me and how they touched me, how they made me feel. I liked how much feeling I seemed to stir in them. Maybe what we'd built between us wouldn't mean much in the outside world, but why shouldn't I find that out rather than throwing it away to avoid facing their rejection? I was braver than *that*, wasn't I?

I had to quit running scared from everyone—from Roseborne's staff, from the guys who'd come to my aid, and from Cade's dire warnings. Cade had said they'd never understand, that they'd turn their backs on me if they saw who I really was. If he'd been right and not just trying to manipulate me into following his lead, I could find that out pretty quickly.

Especially since I wasn't totally sure what I was going to do with this axe once it was sharpened. Chop through the padlocked door? Behead the dean and the professors? Somehow I didn't think either of those plans would get me very far. The tickle of inner power I'd started to feel climbing trees with Elias had stayed with me, but it wasn't giving me any guidance.

I stopped and studied the axe blade, testing it with my finger. Yeah, that definitely had more bite than before. The one thing I did know for sure was that the twisted rosebush in the basement wasn't skewering me this time. I'd be the one slicing through it.

I wasn't going to bring the axe into the school just yet, considering what had happened to my other tools. I tucked it into a narrow space beside the door's hinges and headed out to see what kind of peace I could make.

Evening was falling outside, a purple cast coloring the clouds. The breeze had gotten chillier. Before I went inside, I loped across the lawn and along the wall until I found Violet's rose beneath its jar.

The petals didn't look any more crinkled than they had when I'd planted it, as far as I could tell. Maybe my strategy was working? I'd have a better idea tomorrow, but for now it was a small relief.

As I came up to the school building, Ryo stepped out the front door. He stepped to the side and rolled his shoulders, his lean chest rising and falling with a deep breath. He looked as if he'd needed that fresh air like a fish needs water.

When he spotted me approaching, his posture stiffened just slightly. He hesitated for a moment and then turned to go back inside.

"Ryo," I said, picking up my pace. "Wait. I—I actually wanted to talk to you. You, and Jenson and Elias too. Properly, not like this morning. I didn't handle that very well."

Ryo's eyes glinted with their golden sheen even in the dim light. One side of his mouth curved upward. I could tell he was still uncertain of where this was leading, but he wasn't eager to walk away from me either.

"A little more talking sounds good," he said, and glanced across the lawn. "Should we hold another carriage house meeting? I can find the others."

Like he had before, the first morning I'd arrived in this cycle. My throat closed up just for a second at the easy generosity of the offer in spite of my coldness this morning. The carriage house was secluded enough, no need for worries about Cade observing us to skew my intentions. And I didn't want to have this conversation in the building in front of me, where any of our classmates might wander by and interrupt.

"Perfect," I said, giving him the best smile I could summon in return. "I'll meet you out there."

A shred of doubt niggled at the back of my mind as I stepped into the dim, leathery-smelling interior of the carriage house. For all I knew, Ryo might decide to skip this conversation and renege on his offer after all. But just a few minutes later, the door's hinges squeaked, and all three of my Roseborne boys slipped inside.

Elias came to join me with the most confidence out of all of them, which made sense considering the intimacy we'd shared just a couple of hours ago. Ryo and Jenson walked over more cautiously, Ryo with a palpably hopeful air and Jenson with his mouth set in a wary line. But they'd come. Without meaning to, I'd done a hot-and-cold routine of my own on them in the past week, and they'd been willing to hear me out anyway.

A little ache formed around my heart. I didn't know what I owed Cade, but I definitely owed these three guys a proper explanation.

I motioned to the bench across from me. "Why don't you sit down? There's something I think I need to explain."

They sat down, Elias with perfect posture, Ryo leaning forward, and Jenson sprawling out his long legs in a pose that would have seemed careless if tension hadn't lingered in his shoulders. "Let's have it, then," he said.

I swallowed the lump that was rising in my throat. "This morning, I thought if I just avoided getting any closer with all of you, I could avoid having to own up to things I've done. But that really wasn't fair to any of us. You deserve to know who you've been helping. And I—"

I couldn't stop my arms from coming up to hug myself. My heart beat faster. "I've been falling for you. All three of you, in ways I didn't really think were possible until now. So I don't want to just give up. But you should be able to decide whether you want anything to do with me knowing everything."

"Trix," Ryo started, his eyes widening.

I held up my hand to stop him. "Just let me say it. I need to."

"Go ahead," Elias said gently. From the things he'd said to me this afternoon, I suspected he could guess at least some of what I was about to admit to. But not the worst parts. I had no idea how he'd react to that.

I looked away from them, my restless feet carrying me a few steps to the left and then back again. My combat boots that had always given me so much comfort barely seemed to hold me up.

Just spit it out, Trix.

"You all know I came here to find Cade, that he's my foster brother, and we've been close for a long time," I said. "That's all true. He's looked out for me since I was seven years old, protected me in so many ways... But I never told you—we haven't only been—years ago, when we were just barely teenagers, he started wanting more than that. We'd make out, and then more, in secret... It'd go on for months, maybe a year, and then he'd decide we should stop, so we wouldn't hook up for a while until he wanted to again..."

I couldn't bear to meet their eyes, so I just kept pacing and hurtling onward. "I can't say I didn't want to too. I *liked* that he kept picking me. There was kind of a thrill to the sneaking around. But at the same time—I don't think I ever really felt like I could say no, not without losing all the other closeness we had. I couldn't reject that without rejecting *him*. I went along with it, but it wasn't anything I'd been looking for. He's always been my brother first in my mind, and if things could have just stayed that way— I probably sound like I was an idiot. I'm just trying to say that what happened with him isn't at all the same as what's happened with the three of you."

"You don't sound like an idiot," Ryo said in a low voice. When I forced myself to look at him, he gazed back at me with a determined intensity I'd never seen in him before. "He was a huge part of your life—of course it was hard to step away or think about things without being influenced by him."

Maybe he would know about that the best out of all of them. I'd thought before that Ryo wouldn't understand because his mind had been warped by the drugs when he'd hurt people. But in a way, I had been under the influence too. Having Cade's approval and affection had been my drug, and my addiction to it had screwed up my perception of what made sense, even right and wrong in the end.

But that didn't mean I wasn't responsible. Like Elias had said about his own actions when he'd been proving himself to his grandfather, everything had been my decision. I could have chosen differently.

"I wasn't just an idiot," I said. "I did something horrible. The last time he broke things off, he met another girl a little while later, and they started dating, and it seemed like things were getting serious. He'd blow off our plans to see her. He'd bring up random things about her that I couldn't compete with… Sometimes it'd be just like old times, we'd hang out and everything would be fine, and then I'd feel him slipping away from me. And I kind of lost it."

My gaze dropped to my folded arms. I hugged myself tighter. "I don't even know why I thought it was a good idea. The next door neighbors had this aggressive dog, and Sylvie would always get antsy when it barked at her if they stopped by the house, and Cade would tease her about it. Maybe a little part of me thought that if I could make her *really* freak out over something like that, he'd realize she was a wimp and get over her, but mostly… Mostly I think I was just pissed off that she was getting so much of his attention, and I wanted to torment her a little."

Had I gotten that vindictive impulse from my possible

great-grandfather? I couldn't displace the blame based on that either.

"Anyway," I said, "my big, stupid, awful plan was to call her from a number she didn't know and tell her to come to this courtyard behind a few stores that I knew would be empty at night. I don't even remember what excuse I made up to convince her. I stole the dog and brought it out there, and when she came into the courtyard I let it loose on her. I didn't even care if it bit her or something. But it was even worse. One of the buildings was a café with a big window overlooking the courtyard, and she freaked out so badly she ran without looking and crashed right into it. The cuts from the glass—I called 9-1-1 while I was getting the hell out of there but—she *died.* Because of me."

"Trix," Elias said in the same gentle tone he'd used before—gentle, but it gutted me like a knife blade. "That *is* awful. I'm not going to tell you it's not. But it was one careless emotional decision, and you couldn't have known it'd go like that."

"I still wanted to hurt her. And it wasn't just her. Cade found out about the text calling her out there and knew someone had set it up, and he was furious, and some guy we hung out with sometimes said a few things that convinced him he'd done it. Cade beat him up so badly he ended up in the hospital for weeks, and I didn't do anything. I didn't say anything. His temper has screwed things up before but nothing like that. And that's when Roseborne found him. He wouldn't have gone off like that if it wasn't for me. He's not a bad person."

"What about all the people who get upset without sending someone to the hospital?" Jenson muttered. His mouth snapped shut when my gaze caught his.

"That's not the point," I said. "The point is I've done shit as bad as anyone here, and you've been thinking I'm special somehow because I don't belong here—but I do. More than he does. Maybe more than other people too. So if that's why you liked me, because you thought I was better somehow, now you know. I'm not going to hold it against you if you're out."

For a second, none of them said anything. Then Ryo pushed himself to his feet. He walked straight to me and took my face in his hands, his golden eyes searching mine. "I don't need you to be better than me," he said. "You're still all the things I fell in love with. I *love* you, and nothing you just said changes that. So if you want to give this… whatever it is a shot, and this isn't just a way of telling us you're done, I'm right here."

I choked up so fast I couldn't blink hard enough to press back the tears. Fuck, I'd meant to be strong and factual and here I was on the verge of bawling.

Jenson and Elias had both gotten up too. Jenson leaned over to kiss the top of my head, slipping a possessive arm around my back. "Forget it if you think I'm going to shun you," he said without a hint of doubt.

Elias squeezed my shoulder. "I'm not going anywhere either. No one here is in a position to judge, Trix. I've seen enough to know there's a hell of a lot more to you—and a hell of a lot of it is good."

My mind couldn't quite process the fact that I'd spilled

everything and none of them had turned away. My chest hitched with a sob I tried to hold in. "Okay. I—I didn't really want to lose any of you. Maybe that's selfish, but—"

Jenson let out a rough chuckle. "Why don't we say it's just one more impressive thing about you that you've got so much affection to spread around? What reason do we have to hash out the practicalities of it now?"

Cade had been wrong. Had he even believed what he'd been saying himself, or had he just wanted to cut me off from the other guys who'd captured my attention, like I'd gone after Sylvie to get him back?

In that moment, it didn't seem to matter. The warmth of their presences surrounding me flooded through me with a rush of fondness and hope—and with that came a surge of energy so potent it practically crackled over my skin.

I could take on the staff. I could take on the whole damn school. Right now, with the trust I'd offered and been given in return, I had the feeling I could manage just about anything.

The thought flitted through my head that maybe I should talk to Cade tonight, give him a chance to hear me out and explain where he was coming from, before I did anything drastic. I shook the impulse away.

I didn't need his authorization to try to destroy this place. I was doing it not just for him but for me and the three guys around me, for Violet, for everyone trapped here.

Roseborne was going to fall.

CHAPTER TWENTY-EIGHT

Trix

The guys followed me out to the maintenance shed. With the tingling of power racing through me, my strides seemed to cover twice as much ground as usual. I grabbed the axe from behind the door and hefted it.

"What are you going to do?" Ryo asked, watching with avid anticipation.

"And what do you need *us* to do?" Jenson added.

I adjusted my grip on the wooden handle, testing the tool's weight, and focused on the thrum of energy inside me—almost like the impression I'd gotten from the basement rosebush, but brighter, more invigorating. My instincts tugged at me.

"I don't think the staff can hold me back tonight," I said. "I'm going to hack their power source into bits. We'll see how well they can keep their hold over the school without it." My gaze slid over my three allies and lovers. "I'm not sure how safe it'll be for you."

"I don't give a damn about playing it safe," Elias said. "Will we get in your way if we come with you?"

"I don't think so. Just give me plenty of room. If the staff try to interfere, get in *their* way as well as you can. I'll try to make this quick."

It was early enough in the night that a few students still lingered on the first floor. I tucked the axe close to my leg as we strode past them to the hall with its portraits. My boots thumped down the basement stairs. As I stepped into the laundry room, the resolve inside me reverberated even more powerfully through my body.

I walked straight up to the wall where I'd been carving my passage before, pressed my free hand to the cool concrete surface, and pushed with all that energy whirling inside me. I didn't know how I knew to do it, but every part of me moved as if there was nothing more natural.

The area around my hand crumbled away into crumbs of cement. As they pattered to the floor in an expanding deluge, one of the guys behind me sucked in his breath in shock.

I pushed harder, and the wall disintegrated faster, a hollow forming as tall as I was and wide enough for me to squeeze through. A pinching sensation shot through my chest—and I was through, my fingers plunging into the darkness beyond.

I stepped through the hole without letting myself hesitate. The sconces flared around the edges of the room on the other side—the room I'd stumbled into before. The malformed rosebush loomed in its center, even more jaggedly ominous than I'd remembered.

A hint of doubt shivered through my gut, but I'd come this far. I *would* see this through.

"Holy shit," Ryo murmured as the guys followed me. I trained all my attention on the bush as I stepped up to it, raising the axe. The plant's unnerving energy washed over me, prickling down to my bones. I gritted my teeth. Then I swung.

The axe's blade chopped through the mass of brambles in front of me. Several thorny branch-ends and the mementos of lost students snagged on them clattered on the floor. And a shout carried from the hall at the other end of the room. Of course my efforts wouldn't have gone unnoticed for long.

The guys dashed around the bush to guard the room's entrance. I swung the axe again and again, hacking through the brambles toward the thing's core. Sweat beaded on my forehead and trickled down my back. More waves of that malicious power hit me, but I didn't let my arms falter or even slow.

I have your power in me, I thought at it. *I'm choosing to use it for something better.*

Love or selfishness, like Professor Hubert had said. Or maybe I'd have said, trust over fear.

A scuffling sound and more yells came from the hall, but I didn't let myself look away from my goal for an instant. The power flowing through me must have protected me from the debilitating pain the professors had used to stop me before. It wouldn't help the guys, though. I had to finish this as quickly as I could.

I slammed the axe into the deeper layers of branches, bits of wood and thorn flying through the air around me. One nicked my cheek with a distant sting.

There. I could see the central stem now, plunging into a crack in the concrete floor. More like a gouge than a crack, really, the surface around it splattered with burgundy stains as if the floor had gushed blood when it'd split open. A stale metallic smell wavered through the sickly rose perfume.

I crouched low and aimed the axe's blade straight at the base of the bush. A heavy thump reached my ears. Footsteps pounded across the floor. Clenching my fingers around the handle, I whipped the axe as hard and fast as I could.

Thunk. Thunk. *Thunk*.

With my last chop, the thickly gnarled stem severed completely. The entire remaining body of the bush creaked and toppled over on its side. It burst into an explosion of wood, leaves, and thorn.

As the bits blasted through the air with a roar of the power the thing had contained, the seven figures of the staff who'd been charging toward me veered. Dean Wainhouse, Professors Hubert and Marsden and all the rest flung themselves into the maelstrom, their expressions taut.

The blast hit them, and their forms quivered. Before my eyes, they blurred between the graying adult appearances I'd gotten to know them in and seven teens in burgundy uniforms I'd only before seen in photographs and hazy memories.

Another of those memories rushed into my head: I was standing in almost the same spot, seven classmates around me, with the only light the flickering of a candle set outside our circle. The others all held their wrists, slashed with deep, angry cuts, over the center of that circle, blood spraying down. The first guy was already swaying as the color in his face drained away. The girl next to me —*Mildred*—raked a knife over her own wrist with a choked sound of pain, did the same to the other arm, and then shoved it toward me. The last one.

In that moment, I wasn't sure. Part of me wanted to flee the room and the welling sense of unearthly power that was creeping over my skin. But a larger part of me knew there was no going back. I'd thrown myself into this, and here I was.

I dragged the blade across my wrist, cutting nearly to the bone. Pain seared up my arm as the blood gushed out. I could barely keep my grasp on the handle to repeat the motion on the other side.

The boy beside me—black hair, big nose, *Oscar*— snatched the knife from me with wobbly fingers and fell to his knees. With all his might, he stabbed the blade into the floor in the midst of the blood.

"Take our blood and theirs, and make us something more!" he called out in a hoarse voice, and the floor rocked beneath my feet—

—and I was standing in the basement of the present again, watching the bottom of the rosebush's stem dissolve around the handle of a knife rammed deep into the floor where it had grown.

Blurs of filmy light darted around me. I caught a glimpse of one with Oscar Frederickson's face. Had the staff lost their solid human forms completely with the killing of the bush?

A groan from the hallway cut off any further thoughts along that line I might have had. My heart lurched. I scrambled around the bloodstained patch of floor to where the guys had been attempting to defend me.

Ryo was on his feet, just helping Jenson up. Elias was crumpled on the floor, his whole body shaking as he tried to push himself up. When I dropped to my knees beside him, I couldn't make out any injuries—but the sight of his face, leached of color and cheeks hollowed, made my pulse lurch again even harder.

He looked like my former roommate Delta had in the few days before she'd wasted away with the dying of her rose.

But I'd seen Elias's rose—aged but living—on the bush that clung to the campus wall. Destroying the bush down here shouldn't have hurt him.

A shriek rang out from upstairs. My head jerked up. Dear Lord, what the hell was going on? Were the staff tormenting the students as much as they could in their last moments?

Elias gripped my wrist. "Go," he said, ragged but firm. "I'll be okay. Go make sure it's done."

I forced myself to pull away from him with a tearing sensation in my chest. "We'll look after him," Ryo said with a determined nod. I raced back toward the hole to the laundry room.

The building trembled around me as I hurried up the stairs. Another scream pierced the air—from outside. I raced across the foyer and burst through the front doors. There, I halted in my tracks, my legs jarring.

Our classmates must have realized something had changed. Several of them had run to the gate. But even with all of them hauling at the wrought-iron bars, it wasn't budging.

And farther away along the wall, where the red blooms of the roses showed against the green leaves even in the twilight, ghostly bodies were forming. They congealed in the air in the midst of an eerie fog that gusted from the bush—congealed and began to tramp across the lawn toward the school. A startled cry of my own snagged in my throat.

Destroying the twisted plant in the basement hadn't been enough. We were still trapped within these walls. And I might have unleashed something even more horrifying than the torture the beings that ran this school had already put us through.

ABOUT THE AUTHOR

Eva Chase lives in Canada with her family. She loves stories both swoony and supernatural, and strong women and the men who appreciate them. Along with the Cursed Studies trilogy, she is the author of the Royals of Villain Academy series, the Moriarty's Men series, the Looking Glass Curse trilogy, the Their Dark Valkyrie series, the Witch's Consorts series, the Dragon Shifter's Mates series, the Demons of Fame Romance series, the Legends Reborn trilogy, and the Alpha Project Psychic Romance series.

Connect with Eva online:
www.evachase.com
eva@evachase.com

Made in United States
North Haven, CT
15 February 2022

16152098R00171